HONEY MOON

NOT YOUR VALENTINE

by
Sofi Benitez
with Joyce Magnin

Illustrations by Christina Weidman

Created by Mark Andrew Poe

rabbit publishers

Not Your Valentine (Honey Moon)
By Sofi Benitez
with Joyce Magnin
Created by Mark Andrew Poe

Rabbit Publishers
1624 W. Northwest Highway
Arlington Heights, IL 60004

Illustrations by Christina Weidman
Cover design by Megan Black
Interior Design by Lewis Design & Marketing

ISBN: 978-1-943785-76-6

10 9 8 7 6 5 4 3 2 1

1. Fiction - Action and Adventure 2. Children's Fiction
First Color Edition
Printed in U.S.A.

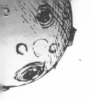

I'd rather eat spiders than dance.

— Honey Moon

Table of Contents

PREFACE

Halloween visited the little town of Sleepy Hollow and never left. Many moons ago, a sly and evil mayor found the powers of darkness helpful in building Sleepy Hollow into "Spooky Town," one of the country's most celebrated attractions. Now, years later, the indomitable Honey Moon understands she must live in the town but she doesn't have to like it, and she is doing everything she can to make sure that goodness and light are more important than evil and darkness.

Welcome to the world of Honey Moon. Halloween may have found a home in Sleepy Hollow, but Honey and her friends are going to make sure it doesn't catch them in its Spooky Town web.

FAMILY

Honey Moon

Honey is ten years old. She is in the fifth grade at Sleepy Hollow Elementary School. She loves to read, and she loves to spend time with her friends. Honey is sassy and spirited and doesn't have any trouble speaking her mind—even if it gets her grounded once in a while. Honey has a strong sensor when it comes to knowing right from wrong and good from evil and, like she says, when it comes to doing the right thing— Honey goes where she is needed.

Harry Moon

Harry is Honey's older brother. He is thirteen years old and in the eighth grade at Sleepy Hollow Middle School. Harry is a magician. And not just a kid magician who does kid tricks, nope, Harry has the true gift of magic.

Harvest Moon

Harvest is the baby of the Moon family. He is two years old. Sometimes Honey has to watch him, but she mostly doesn't mind.

Mary Moon

Mary Moon is the mom. She is fair and straightforward with her kids. She loves them dearly, and they know it. Mary works full time as a nurse, so she often relies on her family for help around the house.

John Moon

John is the dad. He's a bit of a nerd. He works as an IT professional, and sometimes he thinks he would love it if his children followed in his footsteps. But he respects that Harry, Honey, and possibly Harvest will need to go their own way. John owns a classic sports car he calls Emma.

Half Moon

Half Moon is the family dog. He is big and clumsy and has floppy ears. Half is pretty much your basic dog.

FRIENDS

Becky Young

Becky is Honey's best friend. They've known each other since pre-school. Becky is quiet and smart. She is an artist. She is loyal to Honey and usually lets Honey take the lead, but occasionally, Becky makes her thoughts known. And she has really great ideas.

IV

Claire Sinclair

Claire is also Honey's friend. She's a bit bossy, like Honey, so they sometimes clash. Claire is an athlete. She enjoys all sports but especially soccer, softball, and basketball. Sometimes kids poke fun at her rhyming name. But she doesn't mind—not one bit.

Isabela Bonito Stevens

Isabela is Honey's newest friend. Isabela volunteers at the Sleepy Hollow Animal Shelter. Animals are her thing, and she has never met a fur baby she didn't love. Honey is showing Isabela the ropes of living in Spooky Town.

FOES

Clarice Maxine Kligore

Clarice is Honey's arch nemesis. For some reason Clarice doesn't like Honey and tries to bully her. But Honey has no trouble standing up to her. The reason Clarice likes to hassle Honey probably has something to do with the fact that Honey knows the truth abut the Kligores. They are evil.

Maximus Kligore

V

The Honorable (or not-so-honorable depending on your viewpoint) Maximus Kligore is the mayor of Sleepy Hollow. He is the one who plunged Sleepy Hollow into a state of eternal Halloween. He said it was just a publicity stunt to raise town revenues and increase jobs. But Honey knows differently. She knows there is more to Kligore's plans—something so much more sinister.

Nightmare in Gym Class

"**B**oys on this side of the gym, girls on that side." Mrs. Varsity swung an ancient CD player up on a table next to the water fountain.

Honey Moon rolled up the sleeves of her Oxford shirt, staring at her teacher with a puzzled expression. Her best friend, Becky

Young, stood next to her, tugging on her new pony earring. "What is the music for? This is gym class."

"I don't like it," Honey said.

"Yeah," Isabela said. "This is very strange—even for Sleepy Hollow."

"Do you think it's musical chairs?" Becky asked. "I hate musical chairs."

"I don't think so." Honey tried to shove her hands into her skirt pockets, but the pockets were not where they were supposed to be. With a tug, she spun her skirt around so the front was actually in the front. She surveyed the gym. No chairs, no hula hoops, no volleyballs, no jump ropes—just a gym teacher with a CD player. Not a good sign.

The shriek of Mrs. Varsity's whistle shredded the worried voices. All eyes turned toward the gym teacher as she pushed the play button on the CD player. Strains of a waltz wafted through the silent room. A couple of girls couldn't help

2

but sway to the music.

"I thought we'd do something different today," Mrs. Varsity said. A suspicious smile spread across her face. "Since Valentine's Day is a time to appreciate the finer things in life, like poetry, music, and dance . . ."

Honey's eyes flew from the CD player to the line of stinky, immature boys lined up opposite of them. Her lunch burbled.

". . . so find a partner . . ."

3

The entire line of boys took a step backward. Colton slapped his forehead and covered his eyes with his hand. Jacob grabbed his throat and made choking noises. Walker and Aiden pushed Noah forward. "Go ahead," they said. "You first."

He slipped, fell, and crawled back in the line as fast as he could. "No way. Not me."

The girls weren't acting much better. Claire Sinclair glared at Mrs. Varsity. Claire loved sports and wasn't happy about wasting dodgeball time with music. Emily and Madeline ran to Mrs. Varsity and claimed some sudden injury that made it impossible for them to participate.

Someday, in a kingdom far, far away, Honey wouldn't mind dancing with a prince, but there were no princes available at Sleepy Hollow Elementary. Just freckled, smelly elves that mixed gross stuff in their milk cartons at lunch and dared each other to drink it. She would not dance with anyone who'd ever won a burping contest. Not until they were at least thirteen.

"C'mon, guys. Step forward and find a partner or I'll get one for you." Mrs. Varsity tapped her foot in time with the music.

No one moved. Mrs. Varsity grabbed her clipboard and barked out names. "Becky and Jacob, Claire and Logan, Olivia and Aiden, Honey and Noah . . ."

"Lucky," Becky said. "At least Noah is nice. Jacob flips boogers at people."

But Honey didn't feel lucky. Even though the boys and girls were moving toward their partners, no one was actually looking at each other. Instead, they all looked at the gym floor.

Mrs. Varsity stepped to the center of the gym and faced the class. "Now dancers, we're going to learn the box step. Boys first. Start with your left foot. No, left foot. This is your left foot!"

If given the choice between continuing dance class or taking a math test, the kids would've pulled out their pencils and started long division. Instead, with Mrs. Varsity's guidance, the boys scuffed their tennis shoes through the required six steps.

"Good, good! Now ladies, your steps are a little different." Mrs. Varsity took a step backward. The girls learned more quickly. Even Honey picked up the steps with ease, but her stomach churned and her heart pounded at just the thought of dancing with Noah.

"Now for the stance. I need two volunteers."

Mrs. Varsity pointed at Honey and Noah. "You two, come up here."

Honey gasped. She sucked in two lungfuls of air and held it. *No. This can't be happening.*

Her knee sock slid down and puddled around her ankle. "No," she said with her arms tight across her chest. "I can't, Mrs. Varsity. Dancing is against my religion."

"And what religion would that be?" Mrs. Varsity asked. "I could call Reverend McAdams and get his permission."

Reverend McAdams wouldn't save her, not after she broke his office window and interrupted his sabbatical. Her parents wouldn't either. What other excuses did kids use to get out of doing something? Think fast, Honey Moon. Think fast.

"I'm allergic," Honey said. "I'm allergic to boys."

Some of the kids snickered. Aiden fake sneezed.

"Up front, Honey Moon," Mrs. Varsity said. "Now."

Noah gave her a little nudge. "Honey," he whispered, "you're going to get us in trouble. Just do it." Some boys tried hard to get into trouble. But not Noah. Although he often managed to somehow lose homework, rip library books, and break pencils on a daily basis, it was never on purpose.

"Fine, but if you touch me, you die," she growled.

Noah stepped forward.

Honey looked up at the clock behind the cage over the bleachers. How much time left in class? Thirty minutes. She was doomed. But she did as she was told and closed ranks with Noah.

Mrs. Varsity took them each by a shoulder and arranged them facing each other. She grabbed Honey's wrist in her sweaty hand. Honey kept her arm floppy like spaghetti until

Mrs. Varsity tried to put it on Noah's shoulder. Then she jumped like Mrs. Varsity was about to shove her hand into a garbage disposal.

8

"What are you doing?" Honey shrieked.

"You are learning to dance," Mrs. Varsity said. "Someday, you'll be glad you know how."

"No! Never! I'm never dancing with a boy."

"It might be fun," Noah said.

Everyone snickered. Honey's face burned. "This is a waste of time. My parents would never let me dance with a boy."

After school, Honey was in the kitchen helping her mom bake cookies. It was the best place to be on a cold and drizzly February day. The kitchen was warm, the smell of the cookies was delicious, and even the sound of frozen rain against the windows was like music. And that made Honey think about the dance.

"Gym class was so stupid today," she said. "Mrs. Varsity tried to teach us how to dance."

"That's wonderful, Honey. I was thinking I might have to teach you." Mary Moon dumped a bag of chocolate chip morsels into the dough. "So you'd be all set for the big dance."

Honey's jaw dropped open. "The dance? What dance?"

"The Valentine's Day Dance, of course." Honey's mother crooked her finger and scooped a glob of cookie dough out of the mixing bowl. "We'll get you a new dress and fix your hair. You'll look adorable."

"Where is this dance thing? Who's doing it? How do I not know about it?"

"It's done by the Ladies Auxiliary, and it's going to be held at the VFW hall. There are posters about it at the hospital."

"Dad says I can't date until I'm thirty, and now you're telling me that I have to go to a dance? What happened to growing up slowly? What happened to my childhood?"

"It's a dance, Honey, not a wedding." Mary Moon plopped the dough in her mouth. "And you can take all the time you need to grow up."

"I need the time now, during gym class. And

Mrs. Varsity is rushing me."

"What do you mean, Honey?"

"Well, of all the kids in the whole entire class she picked *me* to dance with *Noah*. Like we were two guinea pigs in her terrible social experiment."

Honey's mom let a small laugh escape. "I'm sure she only chose you because she was certain you and Noah would be excellent dancers. And dancing in gym class is perfectly acceptable."

Honey dipped her finger into the cookie dough. "Maybe a hundred years ago when you were in school, but not now. I mean—"

The cell phone on the counter vibrated. Honey's mom grabbed it with her one clean hand. "An email from . . . Mrs. Varsity?"

Honey swallowed. Hard. "I can explain, just—"

Honey's mom lifted a finger—universal mom

11

sign language for stop talking and give me a minute.

Honey coughed on the cookie dough.

"Uhm, she says you told her that you are allergic to boys?"

"Well, I am," Honey said. She dipped her finger into the dough again. "Just looking at their cootie-infested bodies makes me itch."

"And then you told her that dancing was against your religion."

"Just say no," Honey said.

"Obeying your PE teacher is not against your religion," Mary Moon said.

Honey chewed the dough and swallowed— hard—again. "I was hoping."

"Your dad and I expect you to be respectful to your teachers. That means not arguing with them in front of the other students."

12

"But she wanted me to dance. With a boy! With Noah!"

"Who did you want to dance with?"

"No one. I'm not going to the dance."

"You are going, so you might as well learn how to participate. I'm sure your friends Becky and Isabela and probably even Claire are looking forward to it."

13

"Who am I going with? No one is going to ask me."

Her mother wore that annoying know-it-all look that she pulled out for special occasions. "Don't worry. A girl as nice and as smart as you will have a date. I guarantee it."

Honey rubbed her forehead and left bits of unbaked dough in her hair. She was smart, no denying it. As far as nice, well, she did like to help people. Every chance she got she corrected them when they were doing something wrong. She always showed people the right way to act and pointed out mistakes so they could do better in the future. Yes, she was nice. Maybe she was too nice.

"In the meantime," her mother continued, as she scooped out dough onto the cookie sheet. "I have those Valentines we bought on sale last year. You have to have one for each kid in class, remember."

Master disaster. If she gave everyone in her class a Valentine's day card, then of course the boys would think she was nice and would want to ask her to the dance. That must never happen! How could she participate in the Valentine's day party—the cupcakes, the goodie bags, the candy—without planting the wrong idea in the mushy skulls of the boys?

"Where are the Valentine's day cards?" Honey asked.

Honey's mom wiped her hands on a kitchen towel. "Be right back."

If Honey had to, she could probably guess

what kind of valentines they were. Honey lived in Sleepy Hollow, Massachusetts—the town where every day was Halloween night and the only holiday decorations allowed in town had to be spooky in some manner. Never mind that the Headless Horseman was fictional. Never mind that his story was set in New York. People who came to Sleepy Hollow expected to be scared, so the chamber of commerce was happy to terrify.

But in this case, and only in this case, Sleepy   15
Hollow might have done her a favor. Most of the Valentine's day cards sold in Sleepy Hollow already looked like posters from horror movies and were not exactly romantic and mushy.

Zombies saying, "Eat your heart out, valentine."

Spiders saying, "I'm caught in your web."

Skeletons saying, "No bones about it, I want you to be my valentine."

Seeing zombies, spiders, and skeletons at

every holiday got old, but on Valentine's day they represented a safe way to meet the party requirements without declaring your love to a numbskull, fifth-grade boy.

"Here we are." Mary Moon dropped a thin cardboard box on the table just as the oven beeped, indicating it was now preheated to perfect cookie-baking temperature.

"Eight minutes to cookies," Honey's mom said. The oven door creaked on its hinges as she slid the cookie sheet inside.

Honey flipped the red and pink box over and read, True Love 4-Ever—Vintage Valentines from the Heart.

"What?" She shoved the box across the table as far away as she could reach, then sprang back against her chair. "I can't use those. They're . . . they're mushy and sentimental and worst of all—" Honey swallowed, "romantic. Ewwww."

Mary Moon chuckled as she sat at the kitchen table. "Sure you can." She wiped her hands on a dish towel, and chose a card from the box. "Look at this one, Honey. The little boy's legs are so cute and chubby. It says:

> If you could look into my heart
> and see the love that's there,
> And turn it into money,
> you'd be a millionaire.

"Isn't that sweet?"

Honey fake retched. "It's disgusting! And not at all Sleepy Hollow enough. I'm · sure Mayor Kligore would never allow it."

Honey's mom practically dove into the box pulling one card after the other out and reading them. "Oh, these are just precious! Two little naked cupids. It says:

> In summer or winter,
> no matter the weather,
> Heart to heart, dear one,
> we're ever together."

Honey groaned. "There are laws against

17

naked valentines, Mom!"

"How about this one?

Be assured, it's you or none,
That I love and love alone."

Love. Love? Honey thought she might cry. Just imagine Jacob getting that card or Aiden or, worse ever, Noah! She'd never be able to take the spelling bee stage again. She would be forever heckled. "It doesn't even rhyme," she pointed out.

Mary Moon pushed the card into the box and set the box in front of Honey. "All you have to do is put your name on the card, and their name on the envelope. I think you worry too much. No one will take them all that seriously."

Oh, yes, they would. There wasn't a single boy in the class that she could give one of those cards to. Especially now with her mother pushing her to attend the Valentine's day dance.

Desperate times called for desperate

measures. She would find a way out of this predicament.

20

THE ART OF WAR

The school choir room creeped Honey out. Posters of old men with crazy hair covered the walls—men like Ludwig van Beethoven, Wolfgang Amadeus Mozart, and Mick Jagger.

But she took her seat and prepared for music class. She liked music all right—as long as she wasn't being forced to dance to it. Honey noticed Miss Fortissimo staring at her. Oh geeze, what did she do now?

Miss Fortissimo moved closer to Honey's chair and smiled.

"Honey, you have a boyfriend?" Her eyebrows were raised like she'd just heard something unbelievable. "I didn't know you and Noah were . . . an item?"

Honey scowled. An item? What did that mean? Except that even her music teacher had heard about them dancing together in PE class. But how could Miss Fortissimo laugh at her? Wasn't that against some teacher oath they took before they were ever allowed in front of a classroom?

"Honey Moon, Honey Moon, gonna get married soon." Walker's neon soccer jersey swung back and forth as he sang.

Drat her parents and their sense of poetic names.

"I am not getting married, and I don't have a stupid boyfriend!" Each word was louder than the one before until she was shouting. Miss Fortissimo played a chord on the piano that was supposed to quiet them down. Honey gritted her teeth and sucked in a deep breath.

"No reason to yell," Miss Fortissimo said once she could be heard over the laughter. "But even I've heard about you and Noah dancing in gym class."

How do you like that? Ruin one choir performance at the Haunted Holiday Festival and the teacher plots her revenge all winter.

"We weren't dancing. Not together."

"No one would dance with Noah," Aiden said. "He's got cooties."

Noah tugged on the long, straight lock of hair that ran down the middle of his head, keeping his hair from ever being parted straight. He blinked like he was about to cry.

What did he have to cry about? He was the one that said dancing could be fun. A worry started worming its way through Honey's stomach. Maybe he really did like her. Yuck.

Becky, Honey's BFF, elbowed her. "You hurt his feelings," she whispered. "I think he likes you."

Nothing could make Honey like him less. There was no way she would let him think she liked him. He had to be absolutely clear on that.

Isabela, who sat on the other side of Honey, whispered, "Don't let them bother you. You can like whoever you want."

Honey shook her head. "I don't like him—not like, like."

The rest of class dragged on forever. They sang "I Want to Hold Your Hand" by some group named after a bug.

Honey thought the school day would never

end. But, finally, the bell rang, and Honey couldn't wait to get out of the school building and walk home with her friends. Now, she and Becky and Isabela were free to talk—as free as was possible with Claire Sinclair listening in. Claire was a bit of a blabbermouth.

It was a very cold afternoon—even though it was always a little chilly in Sleepy Hollow. This day seemed colder than usual. It never really snowed in Sleepy Hollow since everyday was Halloween night. It was more like autumn all the time. The trees were usually leafless, and the sky was always overcast. And the air smelled of spice and cider.

"Have you got your valentines ready?" Becky asked.

"I do," Isabela said. "Natalie just bought a pack at the Bootique—she was able to find ones with dogs on them, well wolves, but still."

Natalie, that's what Isabela called her new mom. Isabela was newly adopted and was still having a hard time calling her new mother

25

Mom. And that was okay with everybody, although Honey sometimes couldn't resist the urge to butt in.

Honey nudged Isabela. "When you gonna start calling her Mom?"

Isabela shrugged. "I don't know. It's still too hard, but she is starting to feel more like a mom to me."

"That's great," Honey said.

Claire snorted. "My dad bought some last year. All I have to do is write my name on them, and I'm ready to go."

How simple life was for the unsought-after. If Becky was nice, then she might have to worry about boys falling in love with her and inviting her to the dance, but no one would ever ask Claire. She knew karate. And everybody liked Isabela—she was certain to have a date.

Honey adjusted her headband. She hiked Turtle higher onto her shoulders. Turtle always felt just a tad heavier, but not in bad way, when she walked through town. It was like he wanted to remind her that he was with her, walking right alongside her. "My mom has some cards she bought on sale last year. But I don't like them. They're all so mushy. It's disgusting."

"That's why I make my own," Becky said. "That way they say exactly what I want them to say. I'm going to work on them when I get home."

The girls walked on. Honey thought and thought. There must be something she could do to keep Noah or any boy from asking her to the dance. Then, just as they entered the park and Honey got a good look at the Headless Horseman statue holding his pumpkin head, the solution struck her. This was Sleepy Hollow, after all. Why not personalize the cards in a Sleepy Hollow, special kind of way—a spooky way? No one would want to invite her to the dance after she was through. "Can I come over?" Honey asked. "I would love to make my own cards too."

"Sure!" said Becky. "How about you, Claire?"

"No way. I've got a basketball game tonight. You can play with crayons and paste. I'm shooting hoops."

"Suit yourself," Honey said, feeling kind of relieved that Claire was not joining them.

"How about you, Isabela," Honey asked. "Wanna come?"

Isabela kicked at a pebble. "Nah. Not today. Natalie is taking me shoe shopping."

Becky's house wasn't any bigger than Honey's, but it was certainly a lot funkier and a little spookier. Her parents were artists, and they sometimes enjoyed all the Halloween hype. Becky's mom wore homemade jewelry made with stones she polished herself, and her dad liked to wear hemp sandals that showed his hairy toes—something else Honey didn't need to see. If they could braid, bead, grow, or can it themselves, they did. And they had the supplies and tools to prove it.

29

Instead of having a brother or sister to sleep in the third bedroom, Becky had a craft room, and it was the coolest place Honey had ever seen. Roll after roll of wrapping paper, butcher paper, and iridescent, crinkly paper lined the turquoise walls. Shiny silver hooks crowded the white pegboard with at least ten pairs of scissors. Racks full of ribbon spools dispensed a rainbow of satin and velvet. There was even a pottery wheel tucked away in the corner. The room smelled like glue and turpentine, but it wasn't a bad smell. Honey thought it was homey and charming. No wonder Becky's whimsical clothing was often covered in yards of lace and embellishments.

As Becky looked around at all the colorful supplies, Honey thought that maybe a craft room would be better than having a two-year-old brother.

Becky led Honey to a batch of wooden stools crowded around a table that was littered with scraps of leather. Becky shoved the scraps of leather aside.

"What are those?" Honey asked.

"My dad likes to make belts and stuff like that while me and mom do scrapbooking and jewelry." She ducked her head, and smiled up at Honey. "When the three of us are in here working together, well, those are my favorite times."

It was easy to see how a girl could have a favorite time in the magical room, but Honey couldn't imagine her father working in such a girly space. His hobby was restoring his old car.

A 1995 MG-F that he'd named Emma. If he was hanging around fixing something, he was up to his elbows in grease because, as he said, he spent enough time at a desk in a climate-controlled environment. But maybe he needed to get out of the garage. Nothing wrong with having a heater, especially in February.

Becky pointed to a rack of hanging folders. "Here's where we keep the construction paper and cardstock," she said. "It's color coordinated, so we'll probably find what we're looking for in the reds and pinks."

She pulled out a handful of folders, and soon paper with red-and-pink heart patterns was spread across the table. Honey reached to the pegboard for scissors, then paused. There were so many to choose from.

"What color of scissors do you want?" Honey asked.

"It's not the color that's important. It's the pattern. They each cut something different, like scallops, zigzags, and even just plain old

straight edges."

Honey reached on her tippy-toes and brought down a red-handled pair of scissors. Becky wasn't lying. The metal blade swirled in waves. Becky moved about the room like a busy bee flitting from one flower to the next. She knew exactly where every item was— second drawer of the table held hole punches that made hearts, flowers, and arrows. Back to the filing cabinet to grab a folder of paper cut into delicate patterns of lace, then a caddy full of glue, tape, and glue sticks.

Honey never knew there were so many different types of glue or scissors or paper. She might be the spelling bee champion but Becky could teach her a thing or two about arts and crafts.

"Here's a template for making hearts." Becky pushed a plastic cut-out across the table. "Don't you think each card should be a heart?"

Looking at all the cool supplies, Honey could almost grow to love Valentine's day. Just think how creative she could be here! But then she looked again at the heart.

"Are you sure you want to give hearts to everyone?" Honey asked. "Even the boys?"

Becky shrugged. "They won't think anything of it. They're just interested in the candy."

"But what if one of them thinks you like him? He might ask you to go to the Valentine's day dance." Honey was only pointing out the obvious for Becky's own good. She had to see what was at stake here.

33

"I already have a date to the dance." Becky's dark eyes sparkled. She usually was nice to Honey, but now she almost looked like she was laughing at her—just like Miss Fortissimo. "Don't you have a date?"

Becky had a date? Her best friend had a date? With a boy? What was the world coming to?

"No, I don't have a date, and I don't want

one. I told Mom I'm not going. Can you imagine? Dancing with those boys . . . UGH!" Honey pushed the heart template away. "Do you have anything else? Skull and crossbones? A tombstone?"

"I thought you hated the Sleepy Hollow Halloween stuff. I thought you tried to stay away from the scary decorations."

"That's right. I hate the scary decorations. That's why I'm sending them to the boys."

Becky narrowed her eyes. "What if the boys like the scary cards? Then they'll think you're really cool for a girl." She shook her head. "You better think carefully, Honey Moon. You might be walking into a trap."

Honey dropped her head into her hands. What was she doing? Becky was right. If she made a skull-and-crossbones card, they'd be sure to notice. And she did not want to be noticed. Not now, not ever!

"I don't know what to do," she groaned.

Becky slid the heart template back at her. "Start with making cards for the girls. You can make them pretty with no worries."

"Good idea," Honey said. "It'll give me time to think of an alternate plan. I'm quite good at coming up with plans, don't you think?"

"Yes," Becky said. "You're like a mastermind or something."

Becky and Honey cut up an unseemly amount of paper, lace, and ribbons. Becky opened a drawer of stickers—more hearts, puppy dogs, flowers, unicorns, and bunnies. You name it, and there was probably a sticker. Honey plastered several stickers on each of her cards. It was kind of hodgepodge mishmash. Like the sticker drawer threw up on Honey's cards. Then she noticed how Becky only added one sticker per card, and somehow using only one or, at the most, two stickers made her cards look even better. Maybe Becky could teach her a lot.

"This one is to Jasmine." Becky tapped the table with her colored marker. "I think I'll say,

35

'Happy Valentine's day to one of the happiest people I know.' How's that sound?"

Come to think of it, Jasmine was a happy person. Honey knew that for sure. But she never did very well on tests. Not like Honey. Honey always got good grades—straight As most of the time.

Now it was Honey's turn. What could she say on Jasmine's card? Honey took a red pencil and wrote in her best cursive: Dear Jasmine, You might not make good grades, but you don't let it bother you. Happy Valentine's Day.

Becky pulled the card out of her hand. "No, Honey. You can't say that."

"Why not? I'm being nice."

"That's not nice."

"Sure it is. You said she was happy. That's what I'm saying. I'm proud of her for being happy. If I made grades as bad as hers, I'd hate myself. I don't know how she does it."

Becky closed her eyes. "Even if you mean for the words to be nice, you can't say it that way. You said she doesn't make good grades. It doesn't matter what you say after that, you've already hurt her feelings."

Honey rolled her eyes. "She knows she doesn't make good grades. It's not a surprise."

But Becky wasn't budging.

"Fine," Honey said. She pulled the white square of paper off the middle of the card to replace with a clean one. "I'll say 'dear Jasmine, grades aren't everything. Happy Valentine's day.'"

"Did you write that?"

"Not yet." But Honey's pencil was ready.

"How about 'dear Jasmine, you are nice.' That's all you have to say." Becky smiled. "See, easy peasy, lemon squeezy."

"That's all?" Honey mulled this over. The

31

store-bought cards came already ruined by some silly poem on them, but at least they were finished. Trying to be nice without sounding like a moron was harder than Honey had imagined—even when she was making a card for a friend. Which reminded her of her first problem, what to do about the boys' cards?

"This is fun, Honey." Becky's scissors clipped through the paper. "I wish Claire and Isabela could've come over too."

Claire's card would really be a challenge. "I guess for Claire's card, I could write that she is good at sports."

Becky looked up. "I don't think you understand Valentine's day cards," she said. "You aren't supposed to judge people on what they do good and what they do bad. Just say something nice to them."

"But if you say the same thing to everyone, then it doesn't mean anything."

"Trust me."

And maybe that was why everyone thought Becky was sweet. And maybe that was why every boy in the fifth grade had probably already asked her to the dance.

Honey finished the rest of the girls' cards. She managed to find something nice and simple to say on each one—even Claire's.

Honey and Becky had placed their cards on another smaller table in the room so the glue could dry. Then they started on the boys' cards. Becky jumped right in and started cutting and gluing and dashing off nice words that Honey thought could make Princess Frostine in Candy Land gag. But then, all of sudden, it hit her like a brick.

Hallelujah! She didn't need skulls and crossbones. Maybe she could be rude enough to scare the boys away. Honey rubbed her hands together as she formulated her plan. "Give me some more paper. I'm ready to make the cards for the boys."

40

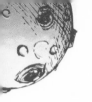

SEALED WITH A FIST

Becky wrote nice things on her Valentine's day cards. Becky was going to the dance where she'd have to dance with an actual boy. Becky had made a big mistake.

Honey wouldn't write nice things in her Valentine's day cards. Honey wouldn't get asked to the dance, and she wouldn't have to dance with any boys.

She finished cutting out and gluing ribbon and putting stickers on the stack of twelve cards for the boys in her class. The glue still gooped out wet on the last ones, but with practice, they looked better than the first ones she'd made. Becky might be right. The boys might not read the frilly cards, but if they did, they would never, ever mistake Honey for a sweet girl who might want to dance with them. Now all she had to do was write something on the inside.

42

Who first? A neon yellow soccer jersey came to mind. Walker.

Dear Walker, Too bad you hit the soccer ball with your head so much. I hope the damage isn't permanent.

She almost wrote Love, Honey, but stopped herself. Instead, she wrote Honey with a small picture of a moon at the bottom. She held it away from her to appreciate the finished card.

Beautiful.

It really was pretty, if you didn't read it. But Honey was counting on the boys reading her cards.

Next one. Dear Jacob, Remember when you drank that milk carton full of pickle juice and ketchup? It made me want to puke. That's what I think of when I think of you. Puked up pickle juice and ketchup. –Honey

What do you know? This was more fun than she realized.

43

Becky lifted her head from the polka-dotted paper she was tracing on. "Let me see your cards."

Honey pushed it into an envelope and sealed it. "It's just like all the others."

"But it's for a boy?" Becky asked.

"Um-hum."

Becky smiled. "Good for you. It doesn't really matter what they think anyway. Noah is probably the only one who would actually read his card. As long as you write something nice for him."

Noah? She couldn't write something nice on Noah's card. Everyone was already putting them in a tree, K-I-S-S-I-N-G. If there was anyone she had to be extra mean to, it was Noah. Otherwise, he might get the wrong idea. Otherwise, he might ask her to the dance, and her mother would make her go. And then her life would be over.

Dear Noah . . .

Honey paused. He was nice. He didn't do gross stuff like the other boys. What could she say that would be honest but would scare him away from ever thinking she wanted to go to the dance with him or, even worse, that she *liked* him?

Dear Noah, You are not as stupid as most boys, but I'd rather eat spiders than go to the dance with you. And I mean it. Stay away! –Honey.

She couldn't get any clearer than that. He couldn't misunderstand now. No way. And hopefully, with no boys in love with her, her Valentine's day would be perfect. At home. Alone.

Becky had given Honey a nice tidy shoebox to hold her valentines. Honey had decorated it to look as Sleepy Hollow Halloweenish as possible. She wrapped it in black construction paper and pasted a skull and crossbones on the top. The hole for the envelopes was right at the skull's mouth. Then she found the worst stickers—barn animals and the planets—and stuck them on the top and on the sides.

45

For now, the box was stuffed deep inside her turtle backpack. She zipped it up and smiled. But Turtle's googly eyes looked away.

When Honey had first seen the backpack while snooping before Christmas, she'd thought it was for her little brother, Harvest. The minute she opened her present was the saddest she'd ever been sitting around a Christmas tree. And the fact that her mother expected her to carry it every day just made it all worse. The fact that she found herself talking to it from time to time was especially worse. But there was just something about Turtle's googly eyes and the way she felt around him. It was definitely weird, but it was also okay with her.

She walked the sidewalk toward her home on Nightingale Lane, burrowing her chin into her scarf to keep out the cold. The scarf muffled her words, but she figured if her turtle were real, it'd have super hearing and could hear her anyway.

"Those boys have it coming. Did you hear how they teased me and Noah about dancing together? I had no choice but to write those nasty cards. It was the only way."

Turtle wasn't talking. She gave it a few seconds, but then, she decided she should probably explain.

"I wouldn't do that if they were nicer and

didn't smell like hamsters and if I wanted to dance. I said nice things in Jasmine's and Emily's cards, didn't I? Even Claire's. Isabela's card was easy. I wrote 'I'm so glad you got adopted.' It's not that I'm being mean. I'm just protecting myself from a fate worse than death—having a boy touch me." She shivered. "I'd rather eat bugs."

She glanced over her shoulder and could see the bright green turtle head bobbing up and down with each of her steps. The motion reminded her of how Mrs. Varsity moved her head to keep time to the music while she and Noah demonstrated the box step in front of the entire PE class.

"Yeah, well, Noah is a nice boy and all that but I still don't want to go to the dance with him. If he understood that, then maybe I could've written a friendly card, but not now. Not with everyone teasing me." She adjusted the straps, which suddenly felt heavier on her shoulders. "Someday he'll thank me for this. Someday he'll realize that I did what I had to do to or else no one would ever stop singing about us and babies in a baby carriage."

And that was the truth.

But she didn't feel any better about it when she got home. Usually talking things out helped. But not this time. On her porch was a cardboard box just about the size of a basketball. Honey grunted when she lifted it. It was a lot heavier than a basketball. She had to juggle it to swing the front door open and dart in before it slammed closed on her. She managed to haul the box into the kitchen.

"Mom, we got a package." The box thudded on the table when she set it down. She slid her backpack off her shoulders and onto the floor. "Where are the scissors?" If this was Becky's house, there'd be a gazillion pairs right at her fingertips.

Her mother came in with Harvest running right at her heels. He wore a dragon mask and snow boots.

Mary Moon pulled a pair of scissors out of

a copper canister on the kitchen counter. "They are here where they always are." She paused over the box. "But that's for Harry."

"Awwww, can't we open it anyway? It might be alive and need some fresh air," Honey said.

49

"No, of course not. Harry will open it when he gets home."

Honey took a deep breath and looked at Harvest, who was busily chomping on a graham cracker he'd found on his chair. "Share?" He held the soggy cracker toward her.

"No, thanks, Harvest," Honey wrinkled her nose. "You know, Mom, I bet Harvest gets lonesome in his room all by himself. We could put him in Harry's room so they could be together."

"We could, but why? We have four bedrooms. We don't need . . ." She looked at Honey, who was smiling from ear to ear. "Oh, let me guess, you have plans for the extra bedroom."

"A craft room with glue, paper, and scissors— lots of different kinds of scissors. And we could put your paints and stencils in there, wrapping paper, glitter. Even Dad could keep his tools in there because working on cars is a kind of a craft."

She smiled. "Your dad likes his tools in the garage. And while a craft room sounds fun, I don't think Harry would appreciate sharing his room with a two-year-old. Would you?"

"Appreciate what?" Harry came into the room from the back. Honey's big brother was thirteen years old and already a bit of a Sleepy Hollow celebrity. Being the best magician in town was like being the best vampire in Transylvania. There was a lot of status involved. Mostly, Harry didn't let it go to his head, and he was usually pretty nice to Honey. Leastways he didn't holler, although he often ignored her lectures. But maybe he'd listen to her now.

"Harry," Honey said, "what would you think about making a room for all of our creative stuff? You know like wrapping paper and coloring books, and you could keep your magic supplies in there."

"Where you or anyone else could see them?" He raised an eyebrow. "No, thanks. A magician's tools are always kept secret. My eyes only."

51

"But you know how you are always clearing the table to make advertisement posters for your shows? We could have a really big table just for painting or drawing or gluing."

Mary turned around. "That reminds me. You got a package, Harry."

"Oh, cool. I've been waiting for this." He turned the box toward him and read the label.

"What is it? What is it?" asked Honey.

Harry ripped the tape off the box and opened the flaps. "Rats."

"What's wrong?" Mary Moon asked.

"It's magic paint, and I need to return it. It was supposed to be black, but they sent green."

"Magic paint?" Honey said. "What's magic about it?"

Harry wrinkled his forehead, which made his short spiky haircut move. "Maybe it paints

pictures for you? Maybe it can fly through canvases? Or maybe, if you paint a rabbit with it, the rabbit becomes real?" He laughed. "A magician never shares his secrets, Honey. You know that."

"But maybe you want to share your room?" Honey couldn't resist one last effort.

Harvest chose that moment to start screaming. "I want to stay with Harry. I want in Harry's room."

53

"Not happening," said Harry.

"But where are you going to put your magic paint? Don't you want a big room to paint in?" Honey asked.

"Why don't you move into Harvest's room and we can paint in your room? How about that?" Harry said.

"I can't. I'm a girl." And she was doing her best to stay away from boys.

54

BURIED ALIVE

I t was a couple of days later, and Honey was feeling pretty good about her valentine booby trap still snug in her backpack. But that feeling did nothing to take her dread of gym class away.

"Do you think we'll have to dance again today?" Honey asked

"Probably," Becky replied. "No one can learn to dance in just one lesson."

Becky readjusted her headband. Her wild brown curls waved crazily in all directions. Her tie-dyed headband was not helping tame her wild mane in the least. That was only one reason Becky could never see the ball coming in dodgeball.

Isabela and Claire caught up with them about halfway to the gym.

"I hope we don't have to dance," Claire said. Claire's blond hair was stretched back tight to make a high ponytail. She wasn't about to let something get in the way of her game, whichever game that might be at the time. "We're supposed to be doing sports for gym. Dancing isn't a sport."

Isabela laughed. "Not a sport? Dancing is just as athletic as basketball or even football. In Ecuador, we have dancers who could probably out run any track-and-field star."

"Awww, I don't care," Honey said. She was feeling quite smug with her plan to sabotage the dance. No date. No dance. And for backup, she knew that one more email from Mrs. Varsity and her mom would say she was grounded. Grounded from the dance? Perfect. Honey was all in.

When they reached the double doors to the gymnasium, they stopped walking and talking. "Not again!" someone yelled from inside. Honey pulled open the door. Music spilled out into the hallway when the door opened.

The students filed inside, and the boys and girls, wanting to make it clear to everyone that they did not like their partners, pooled into separate groups. But not Honey. Honey had a plan. A plan to escape dancing.

With her back against the blue mats that lined the wall, Honey scooted toward Mrs. Varsity's office door. She glanced through the reinforced glass window and saw no escape through there. She arched her back to get around the doorknob, then crept like a ninja to the next door—the equipment room.

"C'mon kids," Mrs. Varsity called. "You know who your partners are. Match up!"

Honey squeezed around the corner into the darkened room. She didn't dare turn on the light. She could hear a little of what was going on outside the room. Mrs. Varsity was taking the roll. Her stomach grew a little wobbly as Mrs. Varsity called each student's name. She had until the Ms to disappear—but how? She was trapped in a stinky equipment room. *What was I thinking?* Honey looked around.

There were the noodles that the boys yelled through until their spit dripped out the other side. She couldn't hide in them. Olivia had thrown up on a yoga mat after the Halloween party. Not to mention blood! The worst. Lots of split lips this year already. Honey stepped around the mats and tried not to breathe too deeply in case they still smelled bad. Could you get sick from smells? A brightly colored parachute hung from a peg on the wall. Honey actually liked the parachute game. On warmer days, the students gathered outside. Each kid grabbed an edge of the parachute making a huge circle and flapped it up and down, up and down, up and down. Once, a giant gust of wind caught it, and the parachute flew over the schoolyard fence. By the time the home owner could retrieve it for them, it'd been smeared with wet dog poop from one of the three Dalmatians that barked at the kids every recess. To this day, the rumor remained that the poop had never been properly dealt with.

No way was she touching that parachute.

Then Honey heard her name called.

"Honey? Honey Moon?"

Silence. Honey knew she could count on her girlfriends not to give her away. But not so much the boys.

"Noah," called Mrs. Varsity, "where is your partner?" The words were muffled by the door but still scary. Honey's time was running out. She opened the lid on the giant coffin of basketballs, volleyballs, and red kickballs. Yes, it was a deep coffin-shaped crate. Good ol' Sleepy Hollow.

Still silence until Aiden called out. "She's here somewhere. I saw her in class."

"Yeah," yelled another voice and then another and another. Honey was really nervous. But also happy, because surely this trick would result in another email from Mrs. Varsity.

60

As Honey heard Mrs. Varsity calling her name, she climbed inside. At first the lid wouldn't close, so she squirmed her way into the thick of the balls, causing a few to topple out. Their bouncing zings echoed in the small closet. She got her legs straight beneath the balls, then lifted those behind her that were keeping her from laying down. Finally, the way was clear. After arranging the balls over her, she reached up and lowered the lid down. A small shiver ran down her back.

The coffin smelled like an odd mixture of rubber and rotting flowers. For the teachers'

Halloween play, they'd had an overweight dummy in the coffin with flowers all around it like at a funeral. At the spookiest part of the play, the dummy popped up and scared the snot out of nearly everyone. Turns out it wasn't an overweight dummy but Principal Chancellor. The teachers thought it was so funny, but that skit had kept the school counselor's office busy all the way through Thanksgiving. It was Christmas before Honey had stopped having nightmares.

And here she was lying in the same box.

There was no way Honey could get the lid to close all the way on account of all the balls. Not enough room for a ten-year-old. The thought of someone pushing it down hard and closing it nearly made her want to jump back out. What if it got stuck? Still, she hoped no one would come in and notice the open lid, especially Mrs. Varsity.

Forty-five minutes. She only had to wait forty-five minutes and then sneak back out and back to her regular classroom. How hard could that be? But the lid rested heavily on the basketballs, which pushed hard into her stomach and legs.

She could still hear her name being called. This time Mrs. Varsity sounded angry.

Honey shifted to the side to give the hardest basketball some more room. She wished they would start the music. The longer they delayed, the more worried she got that her trickery was for nothing. If they played four square after she went through all this trouble to hide, she'd blow a gasket, as her father liked to say.

Turned out that lying on your back in a coffin stuffed with basketballs and dodge balls wasn't fun. Only an NBA vampire could enjoy it. She thought of the Valentine's day vampire display at the flower shop—the pasty-white mannequin in a tux sitting up in a casket presenting a bouquet of long-stemmed roses to whomever passed by. "I love you for eternity," it said above it. She couldn't bear to look in that direction, and here she was in the same position.

Was this what it felt like to be buried? Come to think of it, the coffin smelled more like dirt than rotten flowers. It was damp like she imagined a real grave would be. Honey's heart kicked her in the ribs. And worms. There'd be worms in the casket too. Especially old caskets like this plywood job.

"Honey! Honey!" Now the kids were yelling for her, but at this point, Honey was more worried about the casket than what was happening outside. Had she checked the casket for worms before she got in? Nope. They could be crawling beneath her, even now. Crawling up her arm, digging into her knee socks, burrowing through her hair.

She couldn't take it any longer.

With an impressive shove, Honey threw back the lid and bolted upright. Basketballs and kickballs exploded off her and bounced all over the room. Two bounced so hard they pushed the supply closet door open. From where she sat, still in the casket, Honey saw the two balls bounce right off Mrs. Varsity's feet.

"Honey Moon! What are you doing in there? You come out, right this instant."

And it wasn't just Mrs. Varsity. The entire fifth-grade gym class rushed toward the closet. Some of the kids laughed and pointed as Honey stood in the coffin. She started to climb out when a thread from her knee sock caught on a nail. She pulled and pulled but she couldn't pull it lose.

Becky pushed through the giggling kids to yank Honey's foot free. "What are you doing in

high. Mrs. Varsity dug her short, stubby fingernails into Honey's shoulder and guided her to join the rest of the class sitting in their assigned spots on the floor.

"We've wasted enough class time. Let's dance."

Honey couldn't believe her ears. Seriously? Mrs. Varsity was still going to make her dance after all that, after her coffin caper? "We don't have time now," Honey said.

"Perhaps a visit with Mr. Chancellor would help," Mrs. Varsity said.

"The principal? No. No way. I . . . I'm sorry. But I understand if you have to send an email to my mom."

"Then start dancing."

"How lame," Walker said as Honey walked by. "Hiding in the closet, crying."

"I wasn't crying," Honey snapped. "I just didn't

want to dance with Noah."

Honey caught Noah's eye. He looked away. "It's only the truth," she said.

"The good thing," Noah said, "is that she did manage to waste most of gym class."

That excuse seemed to make sense to her classmates.

"Yeah, that's right," Aiden said. "Good for Honey. Less dancing for us."

Honey felt an invisible smile inside. Maybe they weren't too mad at her, but her mother would be. Hiding out in a coffin filled with rubber balls was certainly grounds for another email. Honey was counting on it.

No Way Out

"Tomorrow's the big day, isn't it?" Honey's father, John Moon, said. He was busy in the garage, polishing his green sports car, a 1995 MG-F. He'd always wanted a car like this when he was younger. The car was old, but Honey's dad often said things that were truly valuable didn't lose their worth over time. It was one of those sayings he repeated every chance he got, until Honey was sure that he was talking about more than a car.

For a minute, she thought he was talking about the dance, so she didn't respond right away.

"Tomorrow is our Valentine's day party at school," she said. "If that's what you mean."

Honey's dad spread more gooey white polish on the roof of his car. "I love a freshly waxed automobile. Look at that shine." Then he looked at Honey. "And speaking of shine. Have you got your cards ready? I bet yours will sparkle away."

Honey nodded. Her cards were ready. She wasn't too sure about the sparkle part—at least not the cards she made at Becky's. The cards were in her room, and if they hadn't already been in sealed envelopes, she might have added a few insults to the boys' cards after today.

"And how about the dance?" Her dad rubbed the driver's side fender a little harder.

Honey leaned against the car. "Well . . ."

"Watch out, sweetie. Don't lean against the paint job. The buttons on your sweater could leave tiny microscopic cracks that would expand over time. It might not show now, but we want this car to look as good thirty years from now as it does today." He waited until she stepped away. "Now tell me about the dance."

Honey felt her stomach wobble. "There is no dance." She rubbed her nose at the dull, sweet smell of the wax her dad was rubbing into the car.

"I'm pretty sure there is," he said.

"Not for me. No one asked me to go," she said.

"Who did you want to ask you?"

"No one! Those boys are gorillas. They might as well sit around and pick fleas off each other. I don't know why Mom insists on me going."

He snapped the rag at her. "C'mon, Honey. Not all of us guys are that bad, are we?"

She would've answered but her mother's car pulled into the driveway. Mary Moon had worn her hearts-and-cupids scrubs to work, but from the look on her face, she might as well have worn a grim reaper pattern.

12

"Again, Honey? Really?" A garment bag from the Bride of Frankenstein formal store dangled from her fingertips.

Honey looked at the dress in confusion. "I don't know anything about that dress."

"I'm not talking about the dress, which will look lovely on you by the way. I'm talking about an email I got from Mrs. Varsity about you disrupting class again. Let me see if I understand this correctly—you spent half of class time hiding in a basketball-filled coffin?"

Honey grimaced. "I did dance . . . once we got all the basketballs put back into the coffin."

73

"I don't understand," her dad said. "Why would you hide during gym?"

Honey stamped her foot. "I just told you. I don't want to dance with boys, and Mrs. Varsity would have forced me to dance with Noah again."

"You know better than to act like that," her father said. "Here I was just thinking about taking you for a ride in the convertible. But your behavior is . . . well it's not good, Honey."

"It sure isn't," Mary Moon said. "I told you if I got another email I would have no choice but to hand down some consequences."

Honey pouted. But it was mostly a fake pout. She was, after all, getting what she wanted. "Okay, Mom, I understand. I guess that means no dance."

"No dance?" John Moon said. "No way. You can still go to the dance. Right, Mary?" Then he winked at Honey's mom. Honey felt her forehead wrinkle. Uh oh. This was not good. This was the worst form of behavior consequences Honey had ever experienced, and she'd experienced a lot.

"You don't want me to go to the dance, do you, Dad?" Honey smiled. "I thought you were supposed to run boys off. Show them your boxing trophies, tell them you work for the FBI, those kinds of things. Instead, you're forcing me to go. What kind of father are you?"

John Moon got a funny look on his face. "Are you worried that no one is going to ask you to go to the dance? Is that what you're really scared of?"

Honey almost leaned against Emma again. "No. I'm afraid someone will ask me, and all the boys in my class are snot-faced numbskulls with—"

"Honey!" her mother interrupted. "You are not being nice."

"They aren't nice to me."

"Is someone bullying you at school?" Mary Moon asked.

Honey's shoulders slumped. "Not really. It's just that, well, ever since Mrs. Varsity made Noah and me demonstrate that stupid box step dance, everyone thinks I like Noah. But I can't stand him. I'm too young to like boys—not like everyone thinks anyway."

"You know what, Honey," her dad said. "I bet Noah feels the same way you do."

"That's not the point. The point is that the boys think I like him, and I don't. But don't you worry. I'll get them back. They'll be sorry."

Her dad held up his hand. "Honey, that's not going to make you happy. Not in the long run. When someone is mean to you, you're supposed to give them kindness in return. Haven't we always taught you that? Love your enemies."

Oh great. More Valentine's day nonsense. She should've put that on their cards. Love your enemies. Happy Valentine's day.

"But if I don't get them back, they'll keep making fun. I've got to do something."

"If your enemy is hungry, feed him. If he is thirsty, give him something to drink." John quoted.

"But that's no punishment," Honey said.

"But it is. Being nice to a bully takes the fun away from them. They can't stand it. Look, you should always tell a grown-up if you're afraid, but don't try to do paybacks."

The hanging bag on her mom's arm ruffled in the wind. "It takes more courage to be nice, Honey Moon. Being ugly is easy. Now, about your behavior at school."

"You're already making me go to the dance. What else can you do?"

Her parents exchanged smiles. It looked like it was her dad's turn to hand down the sentence. "You, Honey Moon, are grounded from the house until dinnertime. You hid during gym class. Now you have to go outside and find someone to play with."

"After dinner, you can try on your new dress," Mary Moon said, "and we'll figure out how we want to do your hair."

"My hair?" Honey slammed her hand on the hood of the car. "You aren't listening to me. I'm not going to the dance."

Her dad's jaw dropped. "Did you just hit Emma?"

Honey slowly lifted her hand away from the hood. From the way her dad acted, Emma was the sister she never had.

"I'm sorry," she said. "I forgot."

Dad got on one knee to eyeball the hood. "I don't see any dents or scratches," he said at last, "but that was close. Next time you might want to just stomp on the ground." He didn't smile, but he did ruffle her hair. "Now go. Play. Run some of that nervous energy out."

Honey thought about stomping her foot on the ground, but it would be a little silly right now. So she just stood there and watched her dad follow her mom inside.

Parents. They never understood.

The door closed behind them, and then Honey stomped on the garage floor with all her might. She wasn't giving in. Those boys didn't

know who they were messing with. They needed to have the fear of Honey in them. What ever happened to justice? To revenge? And, of course, she would feel better if the boys would leave her alone. What were her parents thinking?

80

Oops!

She wanted to scream. She wanted to argue her case more. She wanted to refuse to go to the dance, but now she couldn't even go inside. Honey reached for her bike helmet. Since she was banned from the house, she decided to go find Becky. Maybe she would tell Becky what she really wrote on her cards. Becky would understand why she couldn't dance with boys.

But would she? Honey flung the helmet on the floor. Becky had only seen the cute cards Honey had made. She didn't tell her what she'd written because Becky wouldn't like it. Becky would agree with her parents and tell Honey that she should be nice. That's what Becky would say and that was not what Honey wanted to hear.

She lifted her bike away from the wall. Claire Sinclair. That's who she'd go see. Claire was ruthless. Claire was mean. Claire would agree one hundred percent with what Honey was doing and laugh at the suggestion she should be nice. That's who she wanted to talk to, and she couldn't get to Claire's house fast enough.

Honey threw her leg over her bike and put her foot on the pedal. She would shoot out of the garage like a comet. She stomped the pedal with all her strength but had to swerve around the bike helmet she'd dropped on the floor. The swerve made her go sideways. She

leaned to the left to steady the wheels, but she felt a strange quiver through her handlebars.

Honey knew she wasn't supposed to ride her bike in the garage. There really wasn't room, but sometimes, when a person was mad, they liked to bang things around. Throw helmets, stomp on pedals. No damage done. But this time . . . this time she couldn't keep the bike under control, and it had gone really close to her dad's car. So close that she heard the most terrifying sound in the world. The sound of metal against metal.

83

Honey jumped off her bike, threw it on the lawn, and ran to her dad's car. She crouched down by the wheel and saw it. The biggest, scariest, most gnarly, and jagged scratch ever along the driver's side door. She swallowed. She blinked. She blinked twice. Three times. But blinking didn't make the ugly scar disappear. She rubbed it with her thumb, then with her whole palm. Nothing was helping. All she accomplished was getting flecks of green paint stuck to her sweater. And her dad was worried about her buttons scratching the paint?

This was the worst of the worst. Spouting off to Mrs. Varsity and trying to ditch PE was now small potatoes compared to this. Honey stared at the scratch for what felt like forever. Think fast, Honey Moon. Think fast.

She had to fix it. She was already in deep trouble but this . . . this was so much worse. What could she do? How could she cover up the damage?

Honey took a deep breath. She would even dance with Noah if it would erase the scratch.

Honey scanned the shelves of car wax and cleaners. No paint there. Didn't her dad take the car somewhere to get it painted? Where would that be? Maybe at the car parts store? They sold all sorts of things for cars there. This would've never happened if it weren't for that stupid dance. Her parents didn't even realize how they were ruining her life.

After a bike ride that seemed to last forever, Honey rode up to Ichabod's Auto Supply. The first thing she noticed was a colorful trailer pulled up out front. Logos for WRIP, the local radio station, were plastered all over the trailer that was painted so it looked like dripping blood. Honey shook her head. Even the station's logo screamed Halloween the way it was shaped like a tombstone. Loud voices blared from the speakers. Honey parked her bike beside the trailer. What was going on? She peeked inside the trailer. To her surprise, the bored people sitting in front of microphones looked nothing like the excited voices that were coming out over the speakers. A woman was looking at her phone, her red lipstick even more crooked than the scratch on her dad's car. A man with a tobacco-stained, gray beard was doing a crossword puzzle or something. Honey couldn't really make it out.

"Don't forget to come on out to Ichabod's Auto Supply," the woman recited automatically, "and register to win a year's supply of synthetic motor oil. Stop by and say hi to me, Veronica Dulcet, and my partner, Tyler Jazz."

"Gotta wonder who the lucky winner will be." Tyler rolled his eyes.

Veronica, who looked much more like a Frieda, continued to flip through her phone as she spoke. "Too bad we aren't eligible to win." She really sounded disappointed, even if she looked bored. But Honey had more important things to do than watch the radio DJs. She was just leaving when the woman spotted her. She lowered her phone and slid the window open. "How about an on-air interview?"

Honey shook her head. "I don't feel like it."

"We have nothing going on here." Veronica

tugged on her long, dangling gold earring. "And we have to talk auto parts for another hour. Please, sister. Help us out."

Honey had opened her mouth to say no again, but Veronica was already dragging the microphone off the table and pulling the cords around to reach the little window where Honey stood.

"And now we have a special treat," Veronica said as she put everything in place. "I have a guest here at Ichabod's Auto Supply. Please tell us your name and what grade you're in."

Honey never knew exactly how someone would react when hearing her name, but react they always did. The microphone jutted out the window and waited at her lips like a giant metal ice cream cone that could humiliate her publicly.

"I'm in the fifth grade, and my name is Honey Moon."

Veronica's red lips gawked. "Honey Moon? Like your first name is Honey and your last

name is Moon?"

Honey nodded. "Exactly like that."

Tyler Jazz joined in the fun. "I knew a girl named Anita Bath."

"Rosie Cheeks," Veronica said.

"Peter Pants," Tyler said.

88

"Bella Dance."

Then they laughed like all of this was the funniest stuff on earth.

And these were supposed to be adults? This had to stop. "You can call me Honey," she said. The speakers squawked as her voice erupted over the parking lot.

"Well, Honey," said Veronica, "tomorrow is February fourteenth, so tell us what is your favorite thing about Valentine's day?"

Honey couldn't think of a thing to say. When

she was a kid, everything about school, even Valentine's day, was new and fun, and Honey used to like the cards. It was so exciting to get tons of envelopes addressed to you and you alone. But now that she was aware of the dangers involved, she wished they'd scrap the tradition. The candy was always good but still not worth it. That left . . .

"I don't think our little Honey Moon has much hope for valentines," Veronica said.

"Cat got your tongue?" Tyler asked. "Who's your valentine?"

Honey felt her face go red. As red as a pomegranate, she figured. All she could do was shake her head.

"What's wrong with those fifth-grade boys?" Veronica asked. "Haven't any of them asked you to be their valentine?"

Honey pushed her face right up close on the microphone. "No! I'm not having a valentine. Boys are stinky and gross and they smell bad

after gym class."

Veronica leaned away from the microphone and said in a deep voice, "It doesn't get better when they grow up, either, sister."

"It looks like we have a caller," said Tyler Jazz. "You're on the air with Tyler and Veronica. You wanted to say hello to Honey?"

For a second Honey thought it might be her parents calling. Her parents had grounded her from going inside the house, so they couldn't be mad at her for being on the radio. But it wasn't her parents. It was the sniveling voice of Aiden.

"I just wanted to say that Honey does have a boyfriend. It's Noah. Noah and Honey sitting in a tree . . . "

The hateful song rang out over the mostly empty parking lot and the airwaves of all of Massachusetts.

Honey growled. "Hang up on him."

"Is this true?" Veronica batted her eyes. "Noah is such a nice name."

But Tyler was already shaking with laughter. "Noah Way. Noah Scuse. Noah Ceptions."

Honey grabbed the sliding glass window and jerked it closed, nearly catching Veronica's silver microphone in it. She stomped to the store, ignoring the motorcycle dudes laughing at her.

"I think we made her mad," Veronica said, dripping with fake pity.

"The Honey Moon is over," Tyler said over the speakers.

Oh no, Honey Moon was just getting started. Aiden would be sorry. Just wait. But first she had to repaint a spot on her dad's car. How hard could that be?

92

PROJECT RESTORATION

*D*oesn't she look beautiful? Mary Moon thought. She clasped her hands together beneath her chin and blinked back tears.

Honey felt like crying too, but the tears she held back had nothing to do with her reflection in the mirror.

True, the shiny silver dress made her feel like a princess. True, it floated around her ankles like fairy dreams riding on cotton candy clouds. True, the rhinestones on the skirt caught the light and sparkled like a thousand diamonds. But she wasn't going to the dance. And she had to get dad's car fixed before he noticed it.

Turns out that Ichabod's Auto Parts wouldn't sell spray paint to ten-year-olds. Who knew? Furthermore, when she told them why she needed the paint, the guy behind the counter refused to sell her any kind of paint at all. They even tried to trick her into giving her name so they could call her dad and warn him. Good thing they didn't have the radio on in the store. The whole world knew that Honey Moon was at Ichabod's Auto Parts. They also knew, or thought they knew, that she was in love with Noah.

Couldn't believe everything you heard from the media.

So spray paint wouldn't work, and they wouldn't sell her any touch-up paint. They said

she needed something special. Something professional grade that fifth-grade girls weren't allowed to get their hands on.

"You aren't smiling," her mom said, popping Honey back to the moment. "I thought you'd love this."

Honey fluffed the big sleeves. "I do. I just don't want to go, Mom." This time Honey used her most sincere voice. Because she was sincere. She really didn't want to go.

Her mother bent down and pulled her close. "I'm sorry, sweetie, but your dad and I already decided. Now, why can't you just play along? What's it hurt?"

"It's embarrassing, Mom. How would you feel if someone at work made you get up in front of people and dance?"

"The hospital does have a fancy dance and banquet every year, Honey. And it's true, at first I felt a little . . . awkward, but once I had some practice, the dance became great fun and I

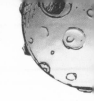

actually look forward to it every year."

Her mom just didn't get it. But Honey couldn't stay and argue any longer. She still had twenty-four hours left to scare off any boy who might ask her to the dance, and hopefully the nasty Valentine's day cards would do the trick. But right now, she had to get out to the garage and patch up Emma.

"Mom." Harry stood at the door to Honey's room. He held the bucket of magic paint.

"I thought you returned that," Mary Moon said.

"Nah. I'm going to keep it after all. The green works just as good as the black."

Honey forgot all about her fancy dress. "Green paint? How is it magic?"

Harry just smirked. "Sorry. Can't say."

"Tell me," Honey begged. "Why can't you tell me?"

"Because you aren't my assistant. Sarah Sinclair helps me."

Sarah was Claire's big sister and their former babysitter. Someday Honey was going to ask her why in the world she wanted anything to do with Harry. Sarah was too cool for a thirteen-year-old.

"Come on," Honey said. "I'll do your chores for two weeks."

Harry only smiled with his best magician's I-got-a-secret smile.

"Okay, kids," their mom said. "It's time to get your showers and get to bed. Tomorrow is your Valentine's day parties and then Honey has the dance."

"Why doesn't Harry have to go?"

"Me?" Harry laughed. "That's the dumbest thing I've ever heard. Of course, I'm not going," Harry said. "And I'm in eighth grade, remember. We don't have Valentine's day parties."

Mary Moon touched Harry's cheek. "Sometimes I forget how grown-up you are."

Harry turned toward his room.

"Hey, where are you taking that paint?" Mary called.

"Back to my room."

"No, sir. That's a disaster waiting to happen. Can you imagine if Harvest found it?"

"Where then? The garage?" he asked.

Mary nodded. "As good a place as any." She smoothed the thick pink sash that wrapped around Honey's waist as she left with Harry. "The garage is definitely a much safer place for goopy stuff."

Honey couldn't take her eyes off the paint can.

"As for you, young lady, get out of that dress and ready for bed. Big day tomorrow."

Honey flopped onto her bed. *What do you know? I needed paint, and I found paint. Green paint.* But just as the thought crossed her mind, Honey got a funny feeling. It was as though someone was watching her. That was when she noticed her turtle backpack sitting on her desk. It kind of stared at her with its googly eyes.

"The green paint just appeared. It's meant to be," she explained to her backpack.

Or was it a test? A test to see how far she'd go to hide her mistake.

Honey glared at the turtle.

"I'm doing this for Dad," she whispered. "I'm being responsible. I'm cleaning up the mess I made."

Or was she trying to avoid trouble? Avoid the consequences?

Honey shook her head. "I have no choice."

Her first impulse was to stomp down the hall, but then she remembered that she needed to be quiet. As she passed the bathroom, she heard the shower running. *Good, Harry is in there.* Then, using her best sneaky skills, she crept down the stairs. She paused against the wall until just the right moment and sneaked past the living room where her parents were watching TV.

She made it through the dark kitchen, shushing Half Moon, the dog, once. And then victory. She made it out the garage door in perfect ninja style. *I'm good. I am sooooo good.*

She eased the squeaky garage door closed and flipped the light switch. And that was when she remembered she had forgotten to change out of her dress. Too late now since she didn't think there was any way she could sneak back inside the house, up to her room, get changed, and then sneak back outside again. She would have to paint the car while wearing her brand-new dance dress.

"It's just a scratch," she said. "I'll be fine."

Even with the poor light, the scratch was obvious. Her stomach wobbled when she saw it. The sound of the bike pedal scraping against the car rushed into her ears. She looked over at her bike hanging on its place on the wall. Stupid bike!

She knelt down to get a closer look at the scratch. The vintage green paint was gone, leaving only a shiny whitish scar that kind of sparkled. Honey smiled. "Put some dark green paint over it and no one will ever know."

Honey stood. *Now where did Harry put that can?* She'd almost placed her now grimy hands on her hips, but even though she was still determined to find a way out of going to the dance, she didn't want to stain the pretty dress. Surely, she'd wear it to some other event.

Honey scanned the garage. There it was. Harry just left the can of paint by the door. "Brothers," she whispered. "No brains."

Now to find a paintbrush.

"Hello," she said when she spied a box on the floor marked PAINT SUPPLIES in black Sharpie. Honey got on her knees, careful to hold her new dress off the ground, and reached into the box. The paintbrush was too broad, but she'd just use the corner of it. Honey gathered the brush and the paint can near the car door. She tried to pry off the lid with just her fingertips, but it didn't budge. Then she remembered how her dad used a screwdriver. She grabbed one from the workbench and dug it into the edge of the lid and *presto* the lid popped off. She set the lid aside and looked into the can. All Honey saw was gooey green. Wonderful, life-saving green.

The paint seemed to shiver in the can, almost like it was trying to get away from the cold air and hide. Like it was alive or something. Honey stirred the top of the paint with the screwdriver—Dad always stirred paint before using it. The paint was thick. Thicker than she'd thought from just looking at it. She scooped some paint onto the bristles and held the brush flat as she brought the brush closer to the car, closer to the scratch, closer to covering her mistake.

She started at one end of the scratch, which

now seemed to loom as large as the Grand Canyon. She held her breath and spread the paint, but the paint looked like the wrong color. It was too light, too bright. Her fists clenched. What had she done? Come on, you're supposed to be magic paint. And just as she thought all was lost, the paint blended into the correct color. Just like magic.

Honey looked at the paint can. But now the paint inside the can looked silver, not green.

Holding the brush close, she squinted at the paint-covered bristles. Silver. *But how? Maybe it's just the poor light in the garage?* She held the brush toward the ceiling, but the light hadn't changed. It was the paint that had changed. Definitely silver. And it wasn't just the color either. Somehow, it'd gotten thin too. Like magic, the thick glob of paint melted and ran into the bristles, disappearing into the thick brush. She'd better get inside the house before her parents found her. One more look at the car, and she smiled. She'd done a good job. At least she hadn't given her parents reason to dole out another grounding.

Something chilled her through her dress. Honey ran her hand over her dress. It was wet. She held her hand up to the light. A shiny silver liquid covered her palm. Paint! And now it was all over her dress.

Oh no. How could her day have gotten any worse? Honey jumped to her feet and flattened out her skirt, prepared for the worse, but true to its magic nature, the paint blended perfectly. Even as she watched, the paint dried, leaving no sign of ever having been on her dress. Honey smiled. Harry sure had the coolest stuff. It really was magic paint. What else would it do? What would it look like if you painted a picture on white paper? Would the paint turn white or did it know what color you wanted it? Just look at how it'd blended with her dress, and the car before that.

The paint on her father's car should be dried by now. Honey turned to where the scratch had been.

"Oh no!" she groaned. The paint on the car was no longer green, but the same silver color

as her dress, and instead of just a thin line there was a wide river of silver that was a hundred times worse than the scratch. Not only that, but the paint was thinner, too, and had run down the side of the car in drippy streaks. The car was a mess. A total disaster.

"No, no, no!" She breathed hard, trying to catch her breath. It was like Claire Sinclair had punched her in the stomach. Fast as lightning, she dipped the brush into the can, careful to scrape it against the side until it didn't drip any more. She painted over the silver as fast as she could. This time, it wasn't just a minor scratch to repair. This time, Honey would have to paint practically the whole driver's side door to cover all the drips. The driver's side! The side her father would definitely see first.

At least the paint was green again. It was like Harry's magic paint could read her mind.

"It'll match," she said. "It'll match." And it did. Once again, the paint made her mistake disappear. When she finished, Honey let out a huge sigh of relief. She just needed to put this crazy stuff away quickly before she could make more messes. Before anything else could happen.

She pushed the paint can lid on as tightly as she could and moved it back to the front of the garage just where the light was strongest.

106

And that's when she saw her dress. The paint she had splashed onto her beautiful princess dress had reappeared. But instead of invisible

silver, her dress was covered in the same sparkly green as Emma. Blotches and squiggles of green were everywhere on the beautiful silver dress. Her princess dress was now a disaster dress. Honey looked at her dress, and her heart sank. *But why do I feel so bad? It's just for the dumb dance.*

Honey tried to shake away the feeling. But she only grew sadder.

Her mom would be so disappointed about the dress. At least her mistake on the car was fixed. She couldn't bear to have both parents upset with her at the same time.

Honey stomped her foot. "I hate this magic paint," she said. She looked around for a place to set the wet brush. She'd better throw it away. It was too dangerous to leave this paint lying around. What if her dad used it to paint something else? She walked around the car to the giant plastic trash can next to the side door. Slowly, she spun the paint brush to keep it from dripping, but the paint was thin, and she had to watch where she was going. By the time

107

she saw the green blob crashing through the air, it was too late. It splashed on her dress, but this time, it hit the pink sash around her waist.

Honey was about to toss the paint brush into the bin, when a large shadow blocked the light.

It was her father. And there she was, wedged between the car and the trash bin. Her heart pounded.

"What are you doing out here in that dress? You'd better get inside before you get it dirty."

Could she go inside? She looked down, and her stomach did a sick double-back flip. The green on her dress had turned pink. All of it. The shiny satin looked like she'd just puked bubblegum snow cone all over it.

And if her dress was covered in pink, then her dad's car . . .

"What in the world?"

He tried to step through the kitchen doorway, but his knee locked, jarring him. Walking like a zombie, her dad was staring at his car. His mouth hung open. Honey was afraid to move.

"What happened?" His voice cracked. "Why is my car pink? Who did this?"

Honey inched her way around the car.

"Did you do this?" John Moon asked.

"I didn't paint your car pink." But in her hand was a giant paintbrush slick with pink paint.

Now would be a good time for her magician brother to make her disappear. "It was an accident. I was really fixing it."

"By covering it in pink paint?"

Her dad reached over the workbench and flipped on a bright light.

Honey sucked in a deep breath and looked at the car. It was worse than she'd thought.

109

"I'm so sorry. I didn't mean to. It was an accident." She said it again in case her dad hadn't heard the first time.

"How do you accidentally paint a car?"

"I did mean to paint it but not pink. It was green—at first."

"What paint? Where? How could you get automotive paint?"

110

"I used Harry's magic paint. And maybe if those guys at Ichabod's would have given me the real car paint none of—"

"Silence," her dad said. "This is no one's fault but yours."

That paint was magic all right. It was magically getting her into more and more trouble.

"When I started, it matched Emma perfectly," Honey said. "I thought it would be—"

"I told you to stay away from my car. Why

would you do this?"

"John." It was her mother. Honey braced herself when Mary Moon appeared in the doorway. Her mother stopped, threw one hand up against the door frame, and slapped the other hand over her mouth. But only for a second. "Your dress! What happened to your dress! Honey Moon if you think that ruining that dress will get you out of the dance, you have another think coming."

"My car," her dad cried. "Did you see my car?"

Now her mother's eyes bulged. "Oh no, young lady. You have crossed the line."

"I didn't mean to." Tears ran down Honey's cheeks. She knew her excuses were pointless. Her bad attitude was the reason the car had gotten damaged in the first place. There was no way to make it better.

"Go to your room," her father said. "I have nothing to say to you right now."

Honey hung her head. She often got in trouble with her parents, but never before had she been in so much trouble that they didn't even know what to lecture her about. This was now officially the worst of the worst. She had not only damaged her father's pride and joy, but she had hurt his feelings also.

"Don't you dare get that paint in your bedroom. Who knows what will happen."

Honey slogged her way to the downstairs bathroom.

A few moments later, her mom appeared with Honey's bathrobe and pajamas. "Change into this and leave the dress. It's ruined."

Honey left the dress lying in the bathtub. She put on her pajamas and cinched her robe. "If the dress is ruined, I guess this means I can't go to the dance," Honey said. Might as well look on the bright side.

But her mom didn't return her smile. "The paint will be dry by then. The dance is still on,

Honey. And you are still going. And you will wear that dress streaked with paint."

114

Put To the Test

Breakfast was quiet. Honey's dad had left for work early. He'd taken her mom's minivan. Yep, she was in bad trouble. Harry had nothing to say except, "I told you to never play with my magic stuff. It's not for . . . for amateurs."

Her mother packed her lunch, not keeping

up the chitchat that usually got them ready for their day. Only Harvest was cheerful, singing some song about a school bus and a kangaroo. When he knocked his sippy cup off the high chair tray, Mary Moon didn't even turn around. Harry picked it up and said, "Spilled juice. Not the same as spilled magic paint, right, Honey?"

Honey thought she might cry again. Never in all her life had there been a disaster like this one. She had hurt three people—she'd ruined the dress her mom bought her, she'd tore up her dad's beloved car, and she'd messed with Harry's magic stuff. All three of them were mad at her—three of her most favorite people in the world. And she had no idea how to make it better.

"I'm sorry I used your paint, Harry," she said.

Harry swallowed some Cheerios. "Okay. You're in enough trouble. I don't need to add to it."

Honey pushed Cheerios around in the milk.

She watched them swirl, and all she could think about was the paint swirling in the can.

"I'm so glad I don't have to do the lame Valentine's day cards anymore," Harry said.

Honey slurped another spoonful of cereal. Even though it wasn't an ordinary day, Honey was glad her brother was trying to keep it normal by picking on her again.

Harry bumped her arm. "How about it? Didn't you make some adorable little cards to give your class?" Then he made kissy noises. And that made her think about the radio show mess-up.

111

The memory still burned. All the magic paint in the world couldn't wash it away. At least she'd finally get to tell Aiden what she thought of him.

"I have cards," she said. "Don't worry about that."

Her mother sighed as she zipped up the

sandwich bag with Honey's PB and J in it. Finally, she turned around. "Honey, you know we love you," she said. "You are in a lot of trouble about the car and the dress, and we'll talk about it when you get home, but I don't want to ruin your party for you."

That was good because Honey had been looking forward to this day for so long. But still, she wouldn't turn away a peace offering, and that was just what her mother was handing her along with her sandwich—a container of heart-shaped sugar cookies covered in pink icing and sprinkles.

"Hey," said Harry, "why don't I get any cookies?"

"Because you're too grown up for lame Valentine's day parties, remember?" Mary Moon said.

Honey still felt sick about her dad's car, but her mom getting the best of her brother made the burden a little lighter.

Harry grabbed his backpack and dashed out the door. "See ya later."

"Have a good day, sweetie," Mary called.

Honey slipped Turtle onto her back. He felt lighter than usual, even with books and Honey's trick valentines tucked inside.

"Bye, Harvest. Bye, Mom."

"Now remember, straight home after school."

119

"I know," Honey said as her mom planted a kiss on her head.

Honey walked a little more slowly than usual even though it was pouring rain. It seemed fitting that it should rain. If only the rain could wash away her feelings and the stains on her dress. Honey Moon had never felt so terrible in her life. Stupid dance. Stupid boys. Stupid party. She only had to make it through today and she'd be home free. One more day without finding a date—or, rather, having a date find her—and then she'd have to miss the dance.

Even her mom and dad wouldn't make her go alone. That thought made her feel better.

Until she got to school.

"I heard you on the radio," Becky said. Her long curly hair was rolled up around her head like a tiara and she wore dangly cupid earrings. "I can't believe Aiden called in."

Claire joined them, her wet tennis shoes squeaking on the linoleum floor. "I'd clock him," she said. "That's what I'd do. I'd clock him for sure."

"Well, that's illegal," Honey answered. "And besides, it really wouldn't help."

"And how must poor Noah feel?" Becky pouted. "If he really does like you, he's got to be embarrassed."

"He does not like me," Honey said. "Mrs. Varsity made us dance together. He didn't pick me, and I didn't pick him. Us liking each other is crazy talk."

"Finally, Valentine's day will be over, and we can stop dancing in gym," said Claire, "and get back to playing real sports."

"But no gym today," Becky reminded them. "We're having a party."

"You should see the cards Honey and I made," Becky told Isabela, who had just joined them. "They are so cute."

Yeah, real cute, until you read them. Honey smiled.

121

Aiden the jerk walked around the corner. Honey froze in her tracks. She didn't want to talk to him, and obviously he didn't want to talk to her. He crinkled up his nose and took off in the opposite direction.

But Claire wasn't about to let him go.

"Hey, Aiden. No use pretending you don't see us."

He turned. "I see you. I just don't want to

talk to you."

"Then why did you call Honey on the phone yesterday if you didn't want to talk to her?"

The noisy hall went quiet. "Aiden called Honey?" someone snickered.

"First Noah, now Aiden," Walker laughed. "How many boyfriends do you have, Honey?"

122 Aiden grabbed Walker by the sleeve. "I didn't call her. I called the radio station to laugh at her."

"That was you?" Walker bent over laughing. "Honey Moon. Peter Pants. Anita Bath."

Honey frowned, but she needed to do something meaner than frowning. The meanest beast she knew was her grandma's Pekingese dog, so Honey showed her teeth and growled like Peaches did every time she walked into her grandma's kitchen.

"Weirdo," Aiden said. Then he lifted his head

toward the other boys. "Let's go."

As long as they kept their distance, she was happy. So far, so good.

Unfortunately, no matter how tough Honey acted, she would still be surrounded by hearts and cupids all day long.

In the classroom, the colorful paper-covered boxes lined the wall beneath the whiteboard. Already her classmates were pacing back and forth with their stack of valentines, matching the name on the envelope with the name on the box.

123

Honey's box was easy to spot with the Jolly Roger pasted on the lid and farm animal and outer space stickers dotting every available spot. The skull looked like it was smiling as people dropped their envelopes into its mouth. Sleepy Hollow perfect.

Honey plopped Turtle on her desk and fished out her cards. The big envelopes might not fit in all the boxes. Oh well. As long as certain boys got them, she'd be happy. As long as certain boys never wanted to speak to her again after reading what she'd written about them, then she'd be more than happy.

Once all their cards were distributed, the students had to settle down and start class, but the morning passed slowly. The girls kept looking at the boxes stuffed full of notes. The boys kept looking at all the snacks. No one was concentrating on reading or adding fractions.

Honey saw the classroom clock strike 2:10. Time to start the party. She felt both excited and a little scared. This could go very, very well or very, very badly.

Isabela got Honey's attention. "This is my first valentine party."

Honey smiled and whispered, "Have fun." But it was Honey who was planning on having the most fun of all when the boys read her valentines.

Mrs. Tenure popped her iPhone onto the speakers and the song "My Funny Valentine"

filtered through the room. The room moms showed up on cue and flew into action. They decorated a table with a red cloth and set plates of cookies and some healthy treats like carrots and ranch dressing around. There were bottles of Hawaiian Punch and ginger ale. All the kids got in line with a pink paper plate.

It didn't take long for most of the treats to disappear. Mrs. Young, Becky's mom, reminded the kids that they could only get one each of the pink cupcakes topped with whipped frosting and conversation hearts, but they could have all the carrots and ranch dressing they wanted. Honey had had all the carrots she wanted, and her plate was empty, but Mrs. Tenure cleared her throat when Honey passed the veggie tray, so she took a few out of guilt.

125

Once everyone had been through the line, Mrs. Tenure set them loose to open their valentine boxes.

Honey dragged herself to the line of boxes. With dread, she popped the box lid off and dumped out the two dozen or so cards.

Several didn't have envelopes—just a card with a cartoon character, a spider, or a skeleton wishing her a happy Valentine's day. She breathed easier with each card she read. So far no one was expressing their love for her. No one was asking her to the dance. In fact, the boys' cards were all store bought and had either Batman or Teenage Mutant Ninja Turtles on them, and they only had a name scribbled down. No message, no thought, just a name . . . and sometimes just an initial. That was all. If only Honey's life was that easy.

"What's yours say? What's yours say?" Jacob hollered to Walker.

The boys were gathered around a desk, shoulder to shoulder, as they read the cards. Then with a burst of laughter, they'd all straighten before someone else announced that they had a card to read.

Apes, that's what they were. They must have made each other funny cards, or more likely, someone bought a package of joke cards. Yeah, that's probably what it was.

The boys roared with laughter again. They were so loud, but at least they weren't paying any attention to the girls' side of the room. That's what she thought until she looked up again and saw them surrounding her desk.

Jacob rested his hand on her desk. Honey recognized the card in his hand, but he didn't look mad. "You think of pickle juice and ketchup when you think of me? Ha! I love it. If only this would've been one of those scratch-and-sniff cards," he said.

Walker held his up. "And you think soccer makes me dumb? That's awesome! I'm going to hang this on my mirror at home."

"We feel bad, Honey. All we did was sign our name on a stupid card," Aiden said. "But you took the time to come up with a joke for each of us. You are so cool . . . for a girl."

"What?" She couldn't believe what she was hearing. "I don't want to be cool. I'm mad at you."

They laughed. "Whatever. Most girls wouldn't ever think to come back with this stuff. It's hilarious."

Honey covered her eyes. This was the worst possible thing ever. She had wanted them to be mad, so mad that they'd never talk to her again. Instead, here they were surrounding her desk like she was one of their gang.

"It's only Noah that's mad," Jacob said. "I don't know what you wrote, but I think you hurt his feelings." The last words were sung in a tattletale voice.

Honey got out of her chair so she could see over the boys' shoulders, and there sat Noah alone at his desk. Now everyone was looking at him. He picked up a card and kept staring at it. His neck and ears turned red.

The only thing Noah had done wrong was be nice to her. It was really Jacob, Walker, and Aiden that she wanted to tick off, but they weren't mad. Her cards hadn't done their job.

"Leave Noah alone," Honey said. "He hasn't done anything wrong."

"Noah and Honey sitting in a tree . . ." It was the same song Aiden had sung on the radio the day before. Before she could stop herself, Honey grabbed a pink cupcake and smeared it right across his face.

He choked and the song ended. Once again, the boys hooted in laughter. Aiden narrowed his eyes at her, then wiped a glob of icing off his face and licked it.

"At least it doesn't taste bad," he said.

"Ewww," the girls chorused.

Then with an ornery glint in his eye he said, "It's sweet. Just like Honey."

This time Honey grabbed her pirate valentine box, but before she could clobber him with it, Mrs. Tenure stepped in and separated them. Aiden went back to the boys' side of the room. Soon, everyone was back to tearing through envelopes looking for candy and discarding the cards that didn't have any message on them.

Everyone except Becky, Claire, and Isabela.

"What was Aiden talking about?" Becky asked. "Did you write mean things on their cards?"

Honey looked at the ceiling. "I wanted the boys to leave me alone. I wanted to make them mad, but it didn't work. It didn't help at all. They all think I'm . . . cool."

"Mean valentines? That's awesome!" Claire punched Honey's shoulder, nearly knocking her down. "I wish I'd thought of that."

"It's not awesome," Becky said. "What if they took her seriously? She could've hurt someone."

"Like Noah?" Stinking Claire had to notice everything. "That was so funny on the radio when they were making fun of his name. Noah Way. Noah Cuse. Noah Ceptions. I was rolling."

They had made fun of Noah's name, too, but instead of feeling sorry for him, Honey had included him in her revenge.

Isabela shook her head. "But the good news is that the dance is tonight. After this, there'll be no more dancing in gym class."

"Are you going?" Honey asked.

"Sure," Isabela said. "Natalie bought me a pretty new dress. I can't wait. And Claire is, too, right?"

131

Claire wrinkled her nose. "My mom says I have to wear a dress. It's so girly and frilly. Ugh."

Honey shot a glance at the boys' side of the room. "Who are you going with, Becky?"

Becky's eyes widened. "You don't know?" She looked at Claire, who winked at her. "Maybe it's a secret," Becky said. "Don't you have a date?"

"No, and I don't want one," Honey said. "That's why I wrote the cards—to keep the boys from asking me." She turned to Claire. "You don't have a date, do you?"

"Of course." Claire swayed and her ponytail swung.

"I can't believe you guys," Honey said. "When did you get boy crazy?"

"It's kind of late to look for a date," Claire said. "You're running out of time."

"I'm not looking for a date!" Honey shivered. "I'm afraid Mom has asked someone because she said I had to go . . . with a boy. I can't figure out who she'd ask, though. Maybe one of Harry's friends?"

"You're just hoping it's Scooter Keys," Claire said.

Honey did believe in miracles, so it was possible that Scooter, an eighth grader, might be going.

"It's not Scooter," Becky said.

Drats. "Do you know who it is?" Honey asked.

Claire and Becky just smiled. Isabela looked like she might burst and spill the beans. But Claire gave her a shoulder punch.

"You know who my date is and you won't tell me?" Honey dropped into her chair. "I'm going to run away from home. At least until tomorrow when this whole thing is over."

But there was someone else slumped in their chair too. Honey knew deep down that she had to say something to Noah. She'd thought she would feel better after telling him how she felt, but instead, she felt awful. She walked to Noah's chair, hoping that everyone would be so busy they wouldn't notice them talking.

133

"I guess you got your card," Honey said, feeling as gross as the gum stuck on the bottom of Noah's desk.

"I was nice to you when everyone else was being mean," Noah said. "Then you go and act like I like you or something."

"You don't?"

"You wish." Noah stared at his desk. "I didn't ask Mrs. Varsity to make us partners."

Honey sighed. Great. Noah hadn't liked her after all. Maybe it was time to start listening to her parents. Maybe she should try to be nice instead of treating everyone like an enemy.

"Okay, I believe you," she said. "You don't like me. Not like-like and that's great. I just wanted to make sure you wouldn't ask me to the dance, but if I have to go with someone . . ." It was a sacrifice, but Noah would probably be better than whomever her mom picked out for her. He looked at her with those big brown eyes that always seemed to be watching her.

"Gross," he said. "You're disgusting. Why would I want to dance with you?"

Hallelujah!

He wrinkled his nose. "And I don't even know what dance you're talking about. Never heard

134

of it. I think you're making the whole thing up."

Once she thought about it, she realized she hadn't seen any posters up at school for the dance. Sure, the Ladies Auxiliary was hosting the dance, but how could they have a dance without boys?

Noah stood up and pushed his desk. It squeaked on the floor. Suddenly, all eyes were on Noah and Honey. Honey dashed away, back to the girls.

135

Was he that clueless? He must be if he didn't realize that she, Honey Moon, had just made him the offer of a lifetime. She was being nice. Making the ultimate sacrifice. But he was not impressed or interested.

Her parents were right. Trying to make people act the way you wanted them to act just didn't work. And no amount of snotty Valentine's day cards could fix some people.

The room moms walked around with large trash bags, and the kids dumped in their trash.

Soon, it was time to gather their cards, snacks, and books and get ready to go home. Honey got her coat.

The Valentine's party had been a disaster. Her cards backfired, and now, it was time to go home and get ready for the dance. But that was nothing compared to what she'd face once she saw her dad. There was still the matter of the painted car to deal with.

Ugh. Honey Moon, you really did it this time.

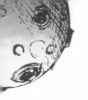

Facing the Music

"I'll see you tonight," Becky said. "Be sure and say hi to my date."

Honey pulled her coat tight and kicked at a pile of wet leaves. She couldn't worry about the dance. Not yet. She had to apologize to her dad. She couldn't rest until he'd forgiven her, but she didn't know how she was going to

make that happen.

All day she'd tried to argue in her head how she wasn't to blame. If her mom and dad hadn't insisted that she was going to the dance, she wouldn't have lost her temper. She wouldn't have gotten on her bike, and the car wouldn't have a scratch. It all went back to them. But then she'd get a sinking feeling in her heart, and she knew she wasn't being fair. Hadn't her dad just warned her to be careful by his car? And then once it got scratched, she should've told them instead of trying to hide it. Honey hated being wrong and hated even more admitting she was wrong, but there was no use in denying it.

The walk home seemed longer than ever. Maybe she wanted to drag it out. She even stood near the Headless Horseman statue for a few minutes.

"You like scaring people," she said. "Harry calls it bad mischief. I guess I did some pretty bad mischief last night, and now I have to face the consequences. Dad says there are always

consequences." Honey tucked some stray hairs behind her ears. She pulled her coat tighter as a cold wind whipped around her ankles. "Guess I gotta face the music."

Honey trudged into her house, but no one met her at the door. Harry was in the living room teaching Harvest how to play Minecraft. Besides them, the house was quiet. Honey let Turtle slip off her back. She held him at arm's length. "Maybe they've forgotten." But when Turtle's googly eyes started to spin like a twister, Honey realized two things. They probably had not forgotten; how could anyone forget such a mess? And two, she needed to fess up and tell her parents her true feelings. Honey pulled Turtle to her chest and squeezed. "You're becoming a good friend."

Honey heard a noise and turned toward the kitchen. She knew that noise. She had heard it the last time she was in trouble. It was her dad, clearing his throat. With a deep breath, Honey stepped into the kitchen. Yep, her dad stood near the garage door. Her mom was sitting at the table.

139

One look at her dad and Honey realized how important it was to get his forgiveness. She couldn't stand for him to be mad. He was too important to her.

Her throat tightened. It was hard to talk. "I scratched your car on accident, and I didn't want you to know," she said, "so I tried to cover it up."

"Why hide it? Were you trying to avoid the consequences?"

Honey stopped fidgeting. Honestly, getting grounded wasn't too bad. Sitting in her room reading books wasn't even punishment, and extra chores weren't terrible, either. That usually meant spending more time helping her parents. Then why did she worry so much about getting caught?

"I guess the real reason I didn't want to tell you was because I'd messed up, and I hate being wrong."

"Do you think you're better than everyone

else?" John Moon asked. "Everyone is wrong sometimes. It's life."

Honey's chin dropped. She might be great at school work, but she wasn't as nice as Becky, as compassionate as Isabela, or as athletic as Claire. And just think how she'd hurt Noah's feelings today. On Valentine's day of all days.

Sometimes, she couldn't do anything right.

"I'm not all that great when I think about it."

141

"Everyone makes mistakes," her dad said. "But when you mess up, it can't just be covered. It has to be forgiven first. If you don't fess up, you're in danger of making the same mistake again and again. And trying to hide it will get . . . well, messy."

Like the car? Like her new dress?

"I'm sorry," Honey said. "I'm sorry for the way I've been acting about the dance. I didn't want to go, and I was mad at you all because you wouldn't listen to me. But I'll go to the dance if you want me to. Just so long as you forgive me for scratching the car."

"I forgive you," her dad said, "but I appreciate the compromise. Agreeing to go with a proper attitude shows that you're trying to make this right." He held out his arms, and Honey gave him a hug.

Her heart felt lighter having this behind them. "I love you, Dad."

"I love you too," he said.

142

"Now grab a bite to eat so we can get you ready. You don't want to be late," said Mary Moon.

"I don't have a dress," Honey said.

"You're wearing the one I bought you."

"The one I spilled paint on?"

"Yep." Her mom took the pot off the stove and drained the pasta.

"It looks—" Honey stopped. Yes, it looked awful, but it was her fault. She wouldn't argue with them anymore. But she did have a question.

"Who's taking me to the dance? You gotta tell me sometime."

Her mom looked at her dad. He smiled. "I'm taking you."

Honey didn't move. On the one hand, not going with a drooling fifth-grade boy was something to celebrate. On the other hand, would everyone think she was a baby if she showed up with her dad? Honey straightened her shoulders. What did she care what everyone else thought? She and her dad would have fun, even if she did look ridiculous in a paint-covered dress.

143

She tried not to think about it as they ate their early dinner. All too soon, she'd finished her meal and asked to be excused. Mary Moon could barely hear her because Harry was going on about the magic paint and the new tricks he could do with it in his magic show. Honey rinsed her plate and cup, set them in the dishwasher, and went to put on her ruined dress.

Too bad the paint wasn't red, she thought. Living in Sleepy Hollow, where every day was Halloween, people would think she'd just splashed blood all over her outfit to fit with the never-ending Spooky Town theme. The dress was hanging from the top knob of her bureau, looking just as pathetic as she remembered. What a pity. It really had been a pretty dress.

She got dressed, the whispery silver material heavy with thick pink paint all down the front. Maybe I'll just wear my coat all night. There weren't rules about dancing in your coat were there? Quickly, she pulled on her tights and shoes, grabbed her hair brush, and went to find her mom, who'd promised her a fancy updo for the night.

The family was still at the table. Harvest's high chair had been cleaned off and he was playing with a little stuffed bunny. This was not Harry's Rabbit. It was a toy. Harvest smiled at

Honey's dress. "Oh, pretty," he said.

Of course, Harvest wouldn't notice the paint, but Harry did.

"What happened?" His eyes grew big. "I knew that you'd messed with my paint, but how did you get that much of it on you?"

"It's a long story." Honey said.

"You can't wear that," Harry said. "Everyone will make fun of you."

"It's okay," said Honey. "I'm used to it."

Harry rested his elbows on the table and covered his mouth. Harvest held the rabbit up to Harry's face.

"Rabbit talks to you." Harvest smiled. "Rabbit wants to talk."

A slow smile spread over Harry's face. "That is magic paint on your dress, right?"

Uh oh. Was she going to get into even more trouble? "Didn't Dad and Mom tell you what I did?"

"I know about the car," Harry said. "Maybe I can help with the dress too—if you want me to."

Honey's heart sped. "Oh, yes, yes, Harry, can you help me?"

He rubbed the rabbit's head and then stretched his hands out before him.

"The magic paint is about to work its magic."

She knew it was magic. It could change colors. But then Harry clapped his hands, and the paint didn't just change colors—it disappeared completely.

Honey gasped. She held out her skirt, and it looked as good as new. Even better, really. Her mom's eyes were shining. Her dad's too, but then he and Honey thought the same thought at the same time. Both of them hurried to the garage.

Dad had already pushed the button to open the big door and let the light in. Honey clapped her hands together and did a few dance steps without even knowing it. The pink paint that had covered the whole side of the car was gone. The metallic green looked like it'd been freshly washed and waxed. It was perfect.

Almost perfect.

Lowering her hands, Honey stepped closer.

The magic paint had disappeared, but the scratch was still there—a deep silver line that couldn't be ignored. She sighed. Perfection was too much to ask.

Her father put his hands on Honey's shoulders. "It would've been nice if that scratch would've gone away too. But sometimes, even when we're forgiven, the damage doesn't disappear. That's going to be something we have to work on before it goes away."

Honey was on the verge of volunteering to work on the car right then instead of going to the dance, but her father spoke first.

"We're not going to worry about this now. My date is all dressed up, and I'm still in my work clothes. I'd better hurry. And I say we take Emma."

And he danced out of the room, whistling a happy tune.

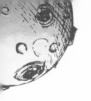

CINDERELLA MEETS
HER PRINCE

Honey had never been inside the VFW hall before. Grandpas went there to play checkers and bingo, and other people went there for anniversary parties with cake, but she had never been invited to either. Honey did notice that the Ladies Auxiliary had decorated the outside for Valentine's day—probably for the big dance. And, in usual Sleepy Hollow fashion, they had put a giant plastic spider out front with a crazy heart on its chest, if spiders had chests, that read I'll Get You in My Web.

There were also black hearts hung from the big maple tree and red and black streamers over the doorway. *Good old Sleepy Hollow*, Honey thought. Her dad pulled the car to the front of the VFW hall. Honey was just about to open the door when her dad pulled the door open. "My lady," he said.

Honey had never felt so grown-up. A gray-haired man wearing a heavy coat smiled at her and took the keys from her dad. Honey watched in amazement as Dad let him get behind the wheel.

"You're going to let him drive Emma?" she asked. "Aren't you worried?"

His eyes sparkled. "I'm not worried. I have my true treasure right here. Now, I believe that

I get to escort you inside." He held out his arm.

Honey smiled as she reached up to take it, just like when they went to weddings and got seated by a groomsman.

Her big skirt swished as she stepped to the doors. Who would be there? Would everyone laugh at her for bringing her dad to a Valentine's day dance?

The VFW hall looked like an enchanted, but spooky, fairyland. A big bubble machine spouted rainbow globes that sailed across the dance floor. Tiny white lights twinkled from the rafters, and bouquets of red and black balloons decorated every corner. But the thing that really gave Honey the creeps was the silly jack-o'-lantern hanging from the ceiling. It spun and cast tiny skulls around the room. Honey shivered and said, "Good old Sleepy Hollow." She always felt better when she said that because it was a way of saying that Sleepy Hollow might still be Spooky Town but she didn't always have to be afraid. She knew the Great Magician that Harry and her mom always talked about was

still in charge, not Mayor Kligore

"There's Mr. Sinclair." Her dad waved to the man wearing the polyester coaches' shorts and embroidered polo with a Jolly Roger over the breast pocket. Honey wouldn't have recognized Claire if it weren't for her ponytail. Her plaid dress—Claire in a dress?—had a black velvet collar that she kept rubbing between her finger and thumb. And she wore a lacy shawl that looked like a spider web.

Honey looked all around. She got an eyeful of Halloween-Valentine's day with the man behind the punch-and-goodies table dressed like Frankenstein and a woman, who looked like Mrs. Varsity, dressed as the Bride of Frankenstein standing next to him. Sheesh. Maybe Claire was meeting her date here? Her father was probably just walking her inside to wait on him. Leaving the dads to talk basketball, Honey pulled Claire aside. "So, who is your date?"

"Don't tell me that you still haven't figured it out." Claire rolled her eyes. "This is a daddy/daughter dance. Boys aren't invited."

"What?" Honey scanned the room but only saw dads, no boys. "You've got to be kidding me. Was it always supposed to be a daddy/daughter dance?"

"Always."

"Then why didn't you tell me? Why did you let me make a fool of myself?"

"I thought you knew at first," Claire said, "but when I realized that you thought you had to go with someone from our class, well, it was just too funny."

153

From across the gym, Becky spotted them. She grabbed Mr. Young by the arm of his leather-fringed jacket and pulled him with her to join them. Becky's simple cotton gown looked like something from *Little House on the Prairie* without the bonnet. Her dad worked at a Whole Foods grocery store and always smelled like dirt. Isabela was wearing a dress she said was true to her Ecuadorian heritage. She wore a bright yellow skirt with what looked like a thousand tight pleats and a wide white belt. Her blouse was frilly and puffy with flowers embroidered all over it. Honey thought she looked spectacular.

"So you found a date after all?" Becky laughed.

"I can't believe no one ever said anything. Especially you." Honey couldn't stop the smile spreading on her face. They'd fooled her, but she was so happy she didn't even care.

"I'm sneakier than you think." Becky wiggled her eyebrows.

Honey shook her head. "Poor Noah. I wrote him and told him he'd better not ask me to the dance. He had no idea what I was talking about."

"He was probably disappointed," Claire said.

"Okay, girls," Honey's dad said. "The music is playing. We'd better get out there and dance so we'll get in some of the pictures and make the moms happy."

Becky, Claire, and Isabela left as Honey took her dad's arm. "I'd like to say I know the box step," Honey said, "but since I spent gym class hiding in the equipment closet, I'm afraid I'm not very good."

"We can be mediocre together," her dad said. He took her hand, put another hand on her back, and began leading her in time to the music. "So, you really thought I was going to make you find a date? C'mon, child. Don't you know me better than that?"

"That's why I was so surprised. I couldn't believe you wanted me dancing with a boy."

155

"Under no circumstances are you to dance with a boy. Not for another twenty years at least. And even then they have to ask for my permission because you, Honey Moon, are priceless. You are my treasure, and I'm guarding you until the right man comes along . . . years and years from now."

"So, if I'm not supposed to dance with boys, what should I do if Mrs. Varsity tries to make me again?"

"Tell her you're allergic."

"Tried that."

"It's against your religion."

"She threatened to call Reverend McAdams."

Her dad looked at the ceiling like he was thinking really hard. "I've got it. Tell her you have to use the phone, call me, and I'll come and be your partner. Every time." With that he gave her a little spin. Her skirt poofed out into a floating circle, catching the light and sparkling the rhinestones.

"This is fun," she said. "But to tell the truth, I don't think I'll do a lot of dancing. Even with you."

"I'm okay with that." He picked Honey up for a final spin as the music stopped.

"Punch and cookies?" he asked as her feet touched the floor again.

Honey and her dad filled their paper plates with heart-shaped cookies

"When should we get started on fixing Emma?" Honey asked as she munched a cookie.

"Soon," John Moon said. "It's more work than you think."

"You don't just paint it?"

"Some mistakes need more than a quick cover-up. You have to make sure you fix the real problem first. In Emma's case, it's a deep scratch, and we have to smooth it out first."

"Ohhh, you have to sand it first?" Honey asked.

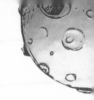

"Of course. It has to be smooth."

The music started again, and everyone moved onto the dance floor.

She'd damaged the car, so her dad probably didn't want her anywhere near it, much less touching it. But if he'd let her do some of the work, she'd feel so much better. "Can I help?" Honey asked hopefully.

158

"I wouldn't have it any other way," he said.

Hello girlfriend,

Wasn't that hilarious? Have you ever been in a similar situation like Honey when you when you made a big deal about something that wasn't even real? Well, I, too, jump to conclusions before knowing all the facts. I guess that just leads me to share something special with you.

Today, I want to talk to you about inner beauty. There's a power that unfolds when you see yourself as beautiful. This world tells us we must fit into a certain expectation of beauty, intelligence, and style. What happens if you can't make the world's cut?

It doesn't mean you get disqualified or become less valuable. What it means is that you are powerful because you understand that your flaws equal uniqueness. Learning to love that uniqueness is more important than basing inner beauty on what others say to you.

Starting today, I want you to see yourself as a masterpiece. This masterpiece has no comparison.

You might ask, "Sofi, how do I see the beauty in my heart?"

My answer is simple. Your actions show the depth of you. Your kindness, your sweetness, your dignity reflect your inner beauty. It takes courage to do no evil. That courage translates to beauty. It's time that girls believe in themselves, shine brightly, and go where they are needed.

Maybe, you don't have the voice of Turtle reassuring you of that today. Let me remind you that you are precious, priceless, and stunning. If you ever feel down, remember you can come to BraveHoneys.com and talk to me. Remember this: we are fearless girls reaching our dreams.

We can't make it on our own, but together we can reach every milestone. We become unstoppable.

Sparkle away.

Love,

Sofi

160

Honey Moon's Super Duper, Crafty, and Tasty Valentine's Day Spectacular!

Hey there, Becky here. I'm so glad Honey asked me to help her. I hope you enjoy these ideas.

First things first. You need craft supplies. The more stuff the better. And, of course, you need your thinking caps and your imagination because, like I always say, anything is possible with a little construction paper, glue, and glitter.

162

FOR THESE CRAFTS, YOU WILL NEED:

- <u>Scissors</u>—Make sure a parent knows you have them. I like the kind that make the fun edges.
- <u>Construction paper</u>—mostly red and white but don't be worried about using other colors too. It's up to you.
- <u>Glue</u> or glue sticks
- <u>Pipe cleaners, paper doilies, lace, tissue paper</u>
- <u>Popsicle or craft sticks</u>
- <u>Googly eyes</u>
- <u>Puff balls</u>
- <u>Felt</u>

- <u>Stickers</u>
- <u>Pretty much anything with a picture or design that you can cut up</u>—like wallpaper samples—I *love* wallpaper samples.
- <u>Mason jars</u>—ask your mom or dad or another adult if you don't have any jars on hand. You can get them in any craft store or even the grocery store.
- <u>Markers, colored pencils, or crayons.</u>
- <u>A couple of the crafts require special supplies</u>, but they're easy to get.

163

SIMPLE VALENTINES

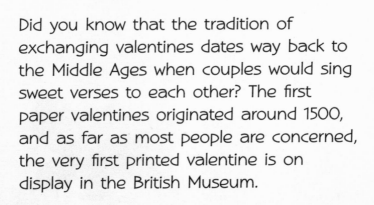

Did you know that the tradition of exchanging valentines dates way back to the Middle Ages when couples would sing sweet verses to each other? The first paper valentines originated around 1500, and as far as most people are concerned, the very first printed valentine is on display in the British Museum.

Easy Instructions:

To make a simple valentine, all you need to do is get a piece of construction paper and fold it in half, like a card. Then you can decorate it however you desire with stickers and cutouts and lace, or even paper doilies.

You can get creative and make your card in the shape of a heart or glue different sizes of hearts onto each other to make it even more special.

Don't forget to write something sweet and sign it with love.

164

Make your own Valentines
or Bookmarks

Supply List

165

- Cardstock—any color
- Red, pink, and purple construction paper to make big hearts
- White doilies
- Valentine stickers
- Glitter—gold & silver
- Markers
- Scissors
- Glue or glue sticks
- Poems (or make up your own sayings)

You can be as fancy as you want or not fancy at all.

1. Start with the cardstock as a base. Make red hearts with construction paper — different sizes/colors. If you want to make fancy cards, glue the hearts on a doily and then glue that to the cardstock. Outline the hearts with glue and sprinkle glitter over it.

2. When the glue is dry, you can add stickers and write a poem or message.

3. For bookmarks, cut the cardstock into rectangular strips. Decorate with stickers and a poem or message.

♥

Mason Jar Candle Holder
or Pencil Holder

♥

These are one of my favorite crafts. If you make a candle holder I recommend you use flameless tea lights. They're soooooo pretty shining through the jar. This craft requires some special supplies so make sure you have everything assembled first.

167

Supply List:

- 1-pint mason jar, cleaned and dried
- Several sheets of white, pink, and red tissue paper
- Elmer's white glue
- Water
- Paper cup
- Paint or sponge brush
- Scissors
- Flameless candle or pencils

Easy Instructions:

1. Cut small squares (1" x 1" or 2" x 2") out of white tissue paper. Then, cut small hearts—any size—out of red and pink tissue paper.

2. In the paper cup, mix glue with water at about a 3:1 ratio until you reach a Mrs. Butterworth's consistency. Just don't make it too watery. Use a sponge or paintbrush to cover the outside of the jar.

3. While the glue is still wet, cover the jar with white tissue paper squares so that no glass is showing. Overlapping squares are okay. Paint over the tissue paper with another layer of glue-water mix.

4. While the glue is still wet, stick hearts to the jar in whatever pattern you want and paint over them with one final layer of glue. Allow to dry, approximately

twenty minutes. Place flameless candle inside jar, and enjoy! Or drop a bunch of pencils inside.

VALENTINE HEART BUTTERFLIES

Supply List:

- Craft sticks, large
- Construction paper or craft foam sheets, any color you want
- Plastic jewels
- Glitter
- Glue
- Small wiggly eyes
- Pipe cleaners

169

Make four small to medium hearts out of the paper or foam sheets. Glue them to the craft stick, two on each side, to make wings. Cut a long, skinny oval for the body, and glue it in the middle, between the wings. When the glue is dry, cut pipe cleaners for antennae and glue one on each side of the body where the top set of wings come together. Glue eyes on the end of the body. Decorate your butterfly with glue and glitter and jewels.

Optional
You can use a wooden clothespin instead of a craft stick so you can clip your butterfly onto a lamp shade or window curtain.

♥

"LOVE IS" MOBILE

♥

I love, love, love this craft. My mom made one for me, and I have it hanging in my bedroom. And it's super simple to make.

Easy Instructions:

1. Cut out one large heart.

2. Cut out eight smaller hearts. Alternate red and white.

3. Using a marker or crayon, on the large
    heart write LOVE IS . . .

4. On the smaller hearts, write one quality
    of love on each heart.
    >Patient
    >Kind
    >Not Mean
    >Not Envious
    >Never Boastful
    >Not easily angered
    >Not proud
    >Not self-seeking

171

5. Cut one piece of yarn about ten inches
    long and fold it in half. Glue it to the
    top back of the large heart like a loop

6. Cut two more strands ten or twelve
    inches long, and glue them to the back
    of the large heart so they hang down
    nicely.

7. Attach the smaller hearts to the yarn.
    Three on the outside and two in the
    middle.

8. Hang it from your ceiling or someplace where you can enjoy it every day.

♥

VALENTINE SUN CATCHER

♥

Supply List:

172

- Clear plastic lids from large yogurt containers
- Felt heart stickers, various colors
- Large needlepoint needle
- Hanging thread or yarn

Thread the needle and push it through the plastic lid near the edge. Pull thread part of the way through, take the needle off, and make a knot. This is the hanger. Then, choose as many hearts as will fit on the lid—two of each size—and stick half of the hearts on one side of the lid. Then, using the exact same size, match them up on the other side. You'll have a sun catcher with the same thing on each side, so it doesn't matter if it you hang it freely from a light or hang it from your window pane.

♥

Valentine Sandwich Cookies

♥

Supply List:

- Vanilla wafers
- Strawberry cream cheese
- Heart candies

173

Spread cream cheese on one cookie and top with another. Put a dab of cream cheese on top and place a candy on it. Serve on a valentine tray or put some in a valentine goodie bag to give away.

Optional You can use plain cream cheese and strawberry or raspberry jam for the middle.

♥
VALENTINE CARD BAG
♥

Supply List:

* Medium brown or white paper bags with handles
* Red, pink, and purple construction paper to make big hearts
* White doilies
* Valentine stickers
* Glitter—gold & silver
* Markers
* Scissors
* Glue or glue sticks

Decorate your bag any way you want. Put your name at the top.

174

♥

A Valentine Bandana for Your Dog or Cat

♥

Why should people have all the fun? Don't forget your pet on Valentine's day. If you don't have any bandanas sitting around (like I do) you can get them at any craft store.

175

Use markers to write something nice about your pet on the bandana or use a paw print stamp to decorate Fido or Captain Fluffy Toe's bandana.

♥

HAPPY HEART POPCORN BOXES

♥

I love sleepovers, don't you? These popcorn boxes are fun for movie time.

You can get the boxes at any craft store, and they couldn't be easier to decorate. Go crazy with the embellishments—that's craft-talk for stuff like hearts and stickers and glitter and sequins and googly eyes and puffballs, pretty much anything.

Don't forget to put each girl's name on her popcorn box.

176

Make Every Day VALENTINE'S DAY!!!

MARK ANDREW POE

Honey Moon creator Mark Andrew Poe never thought about creating a town where kids battled right and wrong. His dream was to love and care for animals, specifically his friends in the rabbit community.

Along the way, Mark became successful in all sorts of interesting careers. He entered the print and publishing world as a young man, and his company did really, really well. Mark also became a popular and nationally sought-after health care advocate for the care and well-being of rabbits.

Years ago, Mark came up with the idea of a story about a young boy with a special connection to a world of magic, all revealed through a remarkable rabbit friend.

Mark worked on his idea for several years before building a collaborative creative team to help him bring his idea to life.

Harry Moon was born. The team was thrilled when Mark introduced Harry's enchanting sister, Honey Moon. Boy, did she pack an unexpected punch!

In 2014, Mark began a multi-book project to launch Harry Moon and Honey Moon into the youth marketplace. Harry and Honey are kids who understand the difference between right and wrong. Kids who tangle with magic and forces unseen in a town where "every day is Halloween night." Today, Mark and the creative team continue to work on the many stories of Harry and Honey and the characters of Sleepy Hollow. He lives in suburban Chicago with his wife and his twenty-five rabbits.

180

BE SURE TO READ THE
CONTINUING AND ENCHANTED
ADVENTURES OF HONEY MOON.

Honey Moon's
DNA

Builds friendships that matter
Goes where she is needed
Helps fellow classmates
Speaks her mind
Honors her body
Does not categorize others
Loves to have a blast
Seeks wisdom from adults
Desires to be brave
Sparkles away
And, of course, loves her mom

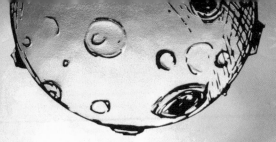

Coming Soon!
More Magical Adventures

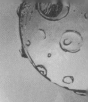

POSTER INSIDE!

HONEY MOON

HONEY FOR MAYOR

VOTE FOR
HONEY
THE *Sheriff's* CHOICE

Keep Voting
KLIGORE!
Spooky too much vs
too no evil

SHERIFF
STATION

SOFI BENITEZ

Harry Moon's
DNA

Helps his fellow schoolmates
Makes friends with those who had once been his enemies
Respects nature
Honors his body
Does not categorize people too quickly
Seeks wisdom from adults
Guides the young
Controls his passions
Is curious
Understands that life will have trouble and accepts it
And, of course, loves his mom!

POSTER INSIDE!

HARRY MOON

TICKLISH

MARK ANDREW POE

FOR MORE BOOKS
& RESOURCES GO TO
HARRYMOON.COM

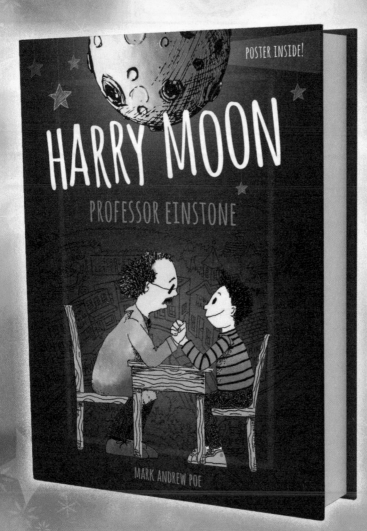

HARRY MOON

PROFESSOR EINSTONE

POSTER INSIDE!

MARK ANDREW POE